LORD HATHAWAY'S NEW BRIDE

HATHAWAY HEIRS

SUZANNA MEDEIROS

LORD HATHAWAY'S NEW BRIDE
First Digital Edition: April 2018
First Print Edition: April 2018
Edited by Victory Editing
ebook ISBN: 9781988223063
Paperback ISBN: 9781988223070

To Jolly Mark, LC Alleyne, Lenore Providence, Lorraine Harding, and Pearl Toy,
For all your inspiration and support over the years.

LORD HATHAWAY'S NEW BRIDE

If he can't have her love, he'll have her passion.

A marriage of convenience…
Sarah Mapleton has already had her heart broken once.
When she finds herself compelled to marry the
intriguing new Viscount Hathaway, she vows to protect
her heart at all costs.

He has her hand…
After unexpectedly inheriting his uncle's title, James
Hathaway discovers that the one thing he wants above
all else is Sarah. He hopes to win her love, but until that
happens, he vows to have her passion.

But can he win her heart?
Sarah is surprised that her new husband can wring
unexpected pleasure from her body. But she realizes too
late that his kindness has also torn down her emotional
barriers. Her determination to protect herself from
being hurt again might have pushed James away
permanently.

∾

To learn about Suzanna Medeiros's future books, you can sign up for her new release newsletter at http://www.suzannamedeiros.com/newsletter

CHAPTER 1

November 1812

*W*AS SHE REALLY going to do this? Marry a man she barely knew... a man who intimidated her more than she cared to admit?

After a lifetime spent witnessing her parents' unhappy marriage, Sarah Mapleton had vowed never to enter a loveless marriage herself. Yet here she was, about to marry a man she'd spoken with on only a handful of occasions.

As she moved into place at the foot of the aisle by her father's side, her gaze centered on her husband-to-be standing at the front of the small church. His back was to the congregation—to her—but she knew what she'd see when he turned around. Triumph. He'd won after all. After initially spurning his suit, here she stood, poised to marry him.

She tried to calm her racing heart, struggled against

the urge to turn and flee. Her father's grip covered her hand like a vise where it rested in the crook of his arm, anchoring her to his side. Panic bubbled up within her when the organ began to play, and following her father's unrelenting lead, she took her first step down the aisle.

Her gaze settled on her mother and younger brother, who were seated in the first pew. Her mother turned to look back at her, and their eyes met. Her mother looked happier than Sarah had seen her in years, and her thoughts began to clear as she remembered why she had finally accepted James Hathaway's proposal of marriage.

After the stress and worry her mother had borne over the past year, stress brought on by how horribly her father had mismanaged their modest estate, Sarah had no choice but to relieve some of that stress by marrying well. She'd agreed to marry the new Viscount Hathaway for her mother's and younger brother's sake. And in doing so had doomed herself.

Welcoming the numbness that descended over her, she forced her feet to move, telling herself that to get through the day, she needed to force down her emotions. But with each step she took, she had to struggle to keep her doubts from surfacing.

Her only consolation was the fact that her instincts about people were rarely wrong, and her instincts told her that the viscount was not a cruel man. No, it wasn't that she was afraid of him, certainly not the way her mother was intimidated by her father. But he was an unknown quantity. A man who exuded confidence and who wouldn't be easily controlled.

She'd learned this past year that she couldn't count on love when the man she'd expected to wed, someone she had known her whole life, had tossed her aside. After that heartbreak, Sarah decided that if she did marry, it would be to someone who'd give her everything she wanted—comfort and security. Someone who wouldn't demand too much of her time and attention. Instead, she was marrying a man who was giving her father everything he desired—his debts repaid and a titled husband for his daughter.

She reached the top of the aisle, and Lord Hathaway turned to face her. She was struck again, as she normally was, by the sheer force of his presence. He was tall—much taller than anyone she knew—and much broader. Some men went to the trouble of padding their coats, but it wasn't even a possibility that the breadth of Hathaway's shoulders was the result of extra material.

The man standing next to her didn't spare her father a glance as he took her hand in his. Instead of the triumph she'd expected to see in his expression, there was heat in his gaze as his dark eyes caught and held hers. For a moment she felt as though she'd been seared, both from the inside and from the touch of his hand through their gloves.

She'd caught glimpses of that expression before, although he usually masked his emotions behind a wall of civility. It came as a surprise that a small part of her, hidden so deep she hadn't even known it existed, responded to that heated glance.

While they stood like that, her hand in his much larger one as they continued to stare at one another, she found herself beginning to lean toward him. Embarrassed by her unexpected and unwelcome reaction to her future husband, she looked away and gently pulled on her hand. She feared he wasn't going to release it, but after a moment he did and they both turned to face Reverend Meeks.

Sarah found it impossible to concentrate on the wedding service. She was trapped inside her own thoughts, chief among them disbelief that she was actually getting married and not to the man she'd hoped to wed. Time and again she tried to force herself to pay attention to what the minister was saying, but the task proved to be beyond her ability.

She lost track of time, and when Hathaway reached for her hand again, she jumped. Something flared in his eyes, but he didn't betray any annoyance as he recited his vows and slipped a ring onto her finger. She stared down at her hand and hesitated before finally collecting herself and repeating her own vows. Somehow she managed to keep her voice even.

When the minister declared them husband and wife, it was impossible to miss the satisfaction on Hathaway's face. In that moment she had to struggle against the constraining feeling that the door of a cage had closed behind her.

THE MORNING of James Hathaway's wedding should have been a happy one. After all, he now had everything a man could desire.

Despite his uncle's best attempts to sire a son, he had died without an heir. Upon his death, the title of Viscount Hathaway had passed to James, and with it had come a great deal of land and wealth.

He hadn't expected to inherit, and so he'd never given more than a passing thought to the title and all that would come with it before his uncle's passing. But the title had gained him the one thing he'd recently discovered he desired beyond all else—his new wife.

Her father, a baronet living near Hathaway Park in Northampton, had paid James a call when he'd taken up residence. Sir Henry Mapleton had made not-so-subtle references to his daughter during that visit, but by that point James had already become accustomed to the seemingly unending parade of mothers and fathers who made no pretense about throwing their unmarried daughters at him. Daughters whom he had no intention of courting.

Then he'd met Sarah Mapleton.

He'd done everything in his power to try to engage her regard, but she'd barely even looked at him whenever their paths crossed—and her father had taken every opportunity to ensure that happened often.

James knew she'd only accepted his suit because her father had pressed her to. He hoped that with time and patience she would come to accept him fully, but as he watched her during the wedding breakfast, it was clear to him that it would not be that day.

The wedding ceremony had been an intimate affair. From his side, there was only his mother and younger sister, his uncle's widow and the man he knew would be her husband when her official mourning period was over. He wished Edward were there, but having recently been promoted to the rank of captain in the British army, his brother was engaged on the continent.

Sarah's immediate family was equally small—her parents and a younger brother, George, who'd come down from Eton for the day. But the wedding breakfast was a different matter. They'd opened the house to friends and neighbors in Northampton, which meant that strangers, few of whom he'd even met before that morning, now flooded several rooms on the main floor of the manor.

Sarah sat next to him during the actual meal, but she'd spoken only a few words. In fact, she'd hardly glanced at him, doing so only when he forced her attention by addressing her directly. From her demeanor when he'd begun to court her, he'd originally thought her shy. He'd since witnessed her several times in other company and had come to realize that she was only reserved with him.

Leaning against one wall of the large dining room, he watched her flit from guest to guest, showing them the outgoing side of her personality that she kept hidden from him. Despite her efforts, he saw enough to realize she was acting a part for their guests. His wife certainly looked the picture of a beautiful, happy bride. Her silk dress of white seemed to shimmer as she moved about the room, her blond curls bouncing as if they, too, had been ordered to appear happy and confident. But he couldn't help noticing that she laughed just a little too loudly, smiled a little too stiffly. He wondered if it was as obvious to everyone else that his new bride would rather be anywhere else than here, celebrating their marriage.

He also didn't miss the way one young man kept looking at Sarah, trying to find opportunities to speak to her, and how she went out of her way to avoid him. Robert Vaughan. James had made it his mission to learn his identity, and it hadn't comforted him to discover that many had once thought he and Sarah would make a love match.

His thoughts were diverted by yet another person demanding his attention. Never good with names under even the best of circumstances, James could have told the portly older man that his effort at currying favor while he was surrounded by so many new faces was unlikely to bear fruit.

After ten minutes of tedious conversation about politics and current happenings on the continent that served only to make him worry more about his brother, James made some vague excuse about being needed elsewhere and went in search of his wife, who had disappeared. Leaving the dining room, he made his way through the other open rooms on the main floor.

He found Sarah in the drawing room, seated on the

settee next to a young woman he didn't know. His wife's posture was stiff, her brows drawn together in a slight frown. Feeling the need to rescue her, he crossed to where they sat on the far side of the room. He was almost upon the pair when the other woman's whispered words reached his ears.

"...can't believe you were actually forced to marry someone so common. He may have inherited the title, but there can be no mistaking that he doesn't come from the same noble stock as the old viscount. How can you stand it?"

He froze in place, waiting to hear his wife defend him. But instead she looked down at her hands, which were clasped tightly in her lap, and shrugged. Disappointment surged within him.

The other woman looked up then and made a strangled noise of dismay. James didn't even glance at her, all his attention focused instead on Sarah. His wife looked up at that moment to see what had alarmed her companion. Their gazes met and clashed.

"It was so nice to have a few minutes to talk to you," the woman said, stumbling over her words and rising with unseemly haste. He didn't look at her as she fled from the room.

Sarah tore her gaze from his and rose as well. He supposed he should have been angry, but given how tense things were between the two of them, he wasn't surprised. He couldn't think of anything to say that wouldn't make the situation worse, and since the room had become more crowded since he'd entered—were

people actually following him?—he murmured something about wanting to introduce her to his mother and
sister. She nodded, managing a small, tense smile for the
benefit of those who were unabashedly watching them,
and took his arm.

CHAPTER 2

IT WAS MIDAFTERNOON when the last of the guests finally departed. With them, it appeared her new husband had also disappeared. Even his mother and sister had left, insisting that they were comfortably settled in the dower house. She found it odd that they hadn't taken up residence in the manor. Heaven knew it was more than large enough. If she hadn't seen for herself the affectionate manner with which her husband treated his family, she would have assumed a familial rift existed between them. But watching them interact, there clearly was no such conflict.

Sarah was grateful for the time alone as she struggled to come to terms with the fact that her life had completely changed. It hadn't helped to see Robert at the wedding breakfast. She had no idea why he'd chosen to attend, but she hoped he hadn't realized she wasn't happy. She didn't want him to know that her heart still hurt when she looked at him.

Avoiding her bedroom lest Lord Hathaway decide to join her there before evening, she decided to explore the house. It was much larger than her parents' modest home. As she made her way to the second floor, she was amazed by the signs of wealth on display everywhere she looked. She'd never been inside the Hathaway manor house before but had expected it to be dark, its walls lined with rich woodwork. Instead, she was surprised to find the house was almost unnaturally light. Pale walls were set off by accents heavy with marble and gilt. The great number of candle sconces everywhere told her the effect would carry over well into the evening.

She'd heard others speak of the former viscount's great wealth, but even though his heir had paid off her father's not-inconsiderable debts, she hadn't quite believed it. She did now.

A footman had told her that the master suites were in the east wing, so at the landing she turned right and headed in the opposite direction. She wandered past many closed doors but ignored them, assuming they were bedrooms that were closed off.

Curiosity led her toward the open door at the end of the hall where light spilled out into the hallway. When she crossed the threshold, she could see why. Tall windows lined one entire wall, and there were no curtains to block the sunlight. The room was long and wide, the wall opposite the windows lined with paintings. Not just paintings—portraits.

She was in the gallery. She knew that manor houses of the nobility often possessed such rooms dedicated to showcasing the family's lineage, but she'd never actually been in one.

Her interest captured, Sarah moved toward the first painting. An inscription below proclaimed it to be a portrait of the first Viscount Hathaway. She was surprised to see that he'd been granted the title less than 150 years earlier. The previous viscount, her husband's uncle, had always seemed so imperious, as though countless centuries of noble blood ran through his veins.

As she examined each of the portraits, she couldn't help but notice the marked similarity in the appearance of the various viscounts over the generations. Every single one of them possessed fair hair and a slim build. There wasn't a painting of her husband, but he was so different that it was almost impossible to believe he belonged to the same family.

JAMES FOUND her in the gallery, frowning at the row of portraits of the previous men who had held his title. His stomach clenched. He knew exactly what she was thinking. He'd hoped never to have this conversation with her, and especially not on his wedding day. But no one had ever accused him of being a coward, and he wouldn't shy away from the truth now.

"I see you've discovered the family's deepest shame."

He winced as the words left his mouth, realizing that they sounded bitter. He'd been aiming for levity.

She turned and waited for him to reach her before replying. "It is a shame to be fair-haired?"

"No, it is an embarrassment that I am not. Something that my uncle never let me forget on those few occasions he deigned to speak to me."

He could almost see her mind ticking away, weighing the implications of his words. His new wife was a clever woman. If she hadn't suspected the truth before, she'd know now. He only hoped she wouldn't be too scandalized.

She licked her lips before she spoke, and he almost groaned at the slight movement. He'd wanted Sarah for his own since first setting eyes on her. It was killing him to exercise restraint and keep his distance in the face of her obvious unease in his presence.

"I was of the belief that illegitimate children couldn't inherit."

He inclined his head. "And you would be correct. My father wasn't illegitimate, but I don't think anyone had any doubt that he and my uncle did not share the same father."

She nodded, apparently accepting his words without censure.

"Your grandmother would hardly be the first woman to bear a child from a lover and raise him together with her other children."

She spoke so calmly that for several moments he was

speechless as he wrestled with the implications of her acceptance. Was it possible she was already with child? Or perhaps she was thinking of the day when she, too, would take a lover. Her ready acceptance of his familial history would certainly explain why she'd agreed to marry him despite the fact that she could hardly seem to stand being in his presence.

Jealousy speared through him at the thought, the emotion so intense and unexpected that he almost recoiled.

"Tell me you're not already increasing."

Color drained from her face at his words, and for a moment, he feared it was due to guilt at his having discovered her secret. The roar of blood pounded in his head. When color seeped back into her face, there was no mistaking that her shock had now turned to anger.

"How dare you accuse me of such a thing." Her lips were pressed together, her chest heaving with indignation as she finished.

It was a struggle to keep his tone even. "You would hardly be the first woman to marry another man after finding yourself in such a condition." He'd deliberately echoed her words, telling her that it was her own fault that he'd come to that conclusion.

Her brown eyes narrowed as she glared at him. "I may live in the country, but I am not a simpleton. Just because I've seen other women behave in such a manner does not mean I come by my knowledge from personal experience."

"So you are not increasing?" The relief coursing through him was immense.

"No," she managed between clenched teeth.

Their tentative camaraderie was now gone, and it was obvious to him that she wouldn't soon forget this conversation. He'd misstepped. Badly. He was supposed to woo Sarah, gain her acceptance of him since he'd never force himself on a woman. Not even his own his wife.

Judging it best to retreat and allow her temper time to cool, he made a swift change of subject.

"I've arranged for you to meet with Mrs. Phillips, the housekeeper. She's waiting for you now if it isn't too inconvenient."

She released a breath, and he couldn't tell if she was trying to dispel her anger or exhibiting her relief that she would no longer have to bear his company.

"Now is fine." She looked down and must have realized she was still wearing her wedding dress. "I'd like to change first."

He nodded and took his leave. She didn't move until he'd left the room, no doubt anxious to ensure he wouldn't follow her to her bedroom.

CHAPTER 3

S ARAH DIDN'T KNOW what to do with herself as she waited for her husband to join her. She had never even kissed the man and now she was about to lie with him. She couldn't help but remember the kisses she'd shared with Robert. She'd believed that he cared for her, but given how casually he'd broken her heart, it was clear she'd been wrong.

The Vaughans were respected within their corner of Northampton, so there had never been any doubt they'd be invited to the wedding breakfast. Incredulity had filled her, though, when she'd seen Robert. Her disbelief had quickly turned to anger, and she'd been tempted to ask a footman to escort him from the house.

In the end, she'd been grateful for the reminder that men couldn't be trusted. The conversation she'd had with Hathaway in the gallery that afternoon had shown her that he felt the same way about her sex. She still found it difficult to believe he'd actually asked her if she was with child. That one question told her that he had a very low opinion of her—perhaps of all women given his family's history. The fact that he'd essentially bought her by agreeing to pay off her father's numerous debts no doubt solidified his low opinion. But then again, their union was no different than that of any other member of the *ton*.

After that brief, uncomfortable meeting in the gallery, she'd spent the rest of the afternoon with the very efficient Mrs. Phillips, who had wasted no time in going over the menus and discussing the running of the household.

She had found it almost impossible to concentrate, her fear of what that night would hold growing by the second as the housekeeper went on about household matters. Sarah hadn't made a good impression with the older woman, but honestly, what had she expected? It was no secret that her marriage wasn't a love match, and she'd wager that any new bride in similar circumstances would be nervous about their upcoming wedding night.

James had seemed content to leave her to her own devices, something for which she was more than a little grateful. Whenever he entered a room, he seemed to take up all the space and she had to keep reminding herself to breathe. She was constantly on edge in his presence. She went to great pains to hide the fact that he made her nervous, but she couldn't tell if her efforts were successful.

When he'd sent word that he wouldn't be joining her for dinner, she'd taken the opportunity to have a tray sent to her room, hoping the time alone would allow her to settle her nerves. It hadn't worked.

She cringed again as she remembered that he'd overheard her cousin offering condolences on her marriage, a sentiment she knew had sprung from her cousin's jealousy and not from true concern. The flash of disappointment she'd seen on his face still haunted her. Of course she hadn't been successful in hiding her reservations from him. She didn't think anyone else had seen through her attempt at a content, if not entirely happy, facade. The fact that he had seen below that surface had unnerved her and served as yet another reminder of how much his mere presence unbalanced her.

When her maid finally left after spending an absurd amount of time fussing over her, Sarah turned toward her new bed. She considered pretending to be asleep, but such a ruse would only gain her an extra day. Perhaps. It was entirely possible Hathaway would wake her.

She started to pace as she considered what was about to happen. In what had been an extremely awkward conversation, her mother had told her that the first night would be the worst. It might be better for her nerves to just get it out of the way. Maybe he'd leave her alone once their marriage was consummated. And if not, she might be lucky and conceive right away. Surely he wouldn't continue to demand his marital rights when she was carrying his child.

She tried not to dwell on his joining her. Much as

she had wanted to avoid the conversation, her mother had gone out of her way to ensure she knew the mechanics of what would happen on her wedding night. Sarah had heard innuendos from some of the staff when they hadn't realized she could overhear them but hadn't been able to piece together herself just what was involved. How was she supposed to bear having a virtual stranger take such personal liberties with her body? Her only hope was that the ordeal would be brief and that he'd return to his own bed after it was over.

Determined not to let fear overwhelm her, she forced herself to stop pacing. She took several deep breaths and tried to push back her racing thoughts.

After her meeting with Mrs. Phillips, Sarah had headed straight to the library to find a book to read. She piled the pillows on the bed and settled against the headboard. Despite her resolve, when she opened the book she could barely concentrate on the words before her. She forced herself to continue, however, determined not to allow her fear free rein.

A shared dressing room connected her bedroom to her husband's. When the soft knock on her door finally came, she lowered the book to her lap with exaggerated care and bade him enter. She gave herself a mental pat on the back when her voice didn't waver.

When he strode into the room, she experienced again the odd sensation that he had taken up all the available space. He still wore the clothes he was attired in that morning for their wedding, but he'd removed the topcoat and cravat. In his shirt and waistcoat, the former open at the throat, the evidence of her husband's muscular physique was undeniable. A strange sensation stirred deep within her at the sight.

Trying to retain her composure, she looked away from him and realized she was holding her book so tightly her knuckles were white. She forced her fingers to relax and made a great show of marking the place in her book before setting it on her bedside table.

Tense silence stretched between them as she searched for something to say. Something that wouldn't reveal just how nervous her husband made her. Even worse, she had no idea what she was supposed to do. Did he expect her to lie there while he joined her? But he'd need to undress first, and if she stayed as she was, she'd witness every moment of it.

Heat rose to her cheeks at the thought, spurring her to scramble from the bed and face him. She would turn around if he started to remove his clothing. She glanced at her bedside table. Should she snuff out the lamp she'd left on so she could read?

When she looked again at Hathaway, she saw his eyes travel down the length of her night rail, lingering on her breasts, then lower. His eyes seemed to burn into her, and embarrassment coursed through her as she looked down to see that the thin garment clung to her uncorseted breasts and wrapped around her thighs. Shocked, she looked up and met his gaze. Hunger shone in his eyes, threatening to steal her breath.

Turning away from him, she came up against her reflection in the mirror of her dressing table. Was that...? She squinted at her reflection. Dear Lord, how had she not realized this garment was quite so sheer? Surely the modiste who'd created it for her wedding night should have said something to her—she could almost see right through it. She covered her face with her hands, mortified that she was virtually naked in front of this man who was little more than a stranger to her.

She heard him move behind her and tensed when the weight of his hands settled on her shoulders.

"You're afraid." She could hear the concern in his voice. "I won't hurt you."

She lowered her hands and crossed them over her breasts, her hands settling just below his on her shoulders. Their eyes met in the mirror.

"We barely know one another. It seems unbelievable that I'm here with you, like this. And I don't know what I should be doing."

"You hate the fact that you're not in control."

She was going to deny it but then realized he was correct. Yes, she was nervous, and yes, she was embarrassed, but what she struggled with most was exactly what he'd pointed out. It was the first night of their marriage together, and she feared that by ceding control to him now, she would find herself on even shakier ground in the future.

His hands covered hers, making her aware of the ring he'd placed on her finger just that morning. Slowly he dragged her hands down to her sides and held them there while his gaze traveled over the reflection of her body.

"You are very beautiful," he said, his voice thick.

She knew she was pretty, but the way he spoke, his voice almost reverential, gave the words extra weight. He wasn't just paying her a compliment... The words sounded as though they had been torn from his very soul. She stared at him in the mirror, unable to look away. When he moved his hands to her waist, she drew in a deep breath. His hands were so hot they seemed to burn right through the thin fabric of her night rail. She might as well have been wearing nothing.

She could only watch in silence, holding her breath and bracing herself for the touch of his mouth as his dark head descended toward the side of her neck. Robert had never done this to her, and she felt powerless, unsure what to do. When her husband's lips touched her skin, she closed her eyes, unable to watch. She was taken aback by his gentleness, his mouth resting against her throat, the heat of his breath causing a shiver to go through her.

When she opened her eyes again, she saw that his eyes were trained on her face in the mirror. He started to inch his hands upward. His palms settled over her breasts, his thumbs toying with the hardened peaks through the fabric, and she let out a shaky breath. The intimacy of his touch was almost unbearable.

"Please," she said, feeling suddenly shy. "I can't watch... It's too much."

He stilled, and for a moment she thought he was going to deny her, but then with a curt nod he shifted their bodies so she was no longer standing in front of her dressing table.

Without the embarrassment of having to watch herself while he touched her, there was only him. Her husband. His large body pressed against her from behind, his hands holding her, one on her breast, the other on her stomach. And oh God, he'd lowered his mouth to her neck again and was doing something wicked with his lips and tongue that caused her to moan and tilt her head farther to the side.

She could feel his hardness pressing into her lower back, and she should have been afraid. She knew what was going to come next, and while her mind tried to prepare her for the pain of his impending penetration, her body seemed to revel under his touch. Without conscious thought, she pressed back into him and a thrill of satisfaction went through her when she heard his groan. He had completely unbalanced her, giving her pleasure when she'd expected none, but she was also having a similar effect on him.

His hands bunched the fabric at her hips, and when he started to drag the material up, she was almost breathless with anticipation at the thought of feeling his warm touch on her skin.

Was this normal? Was she supposed to be enjoying his touch so much?

When he caressed her now-bared thighs and swept one hand between them, she opened for him without having to be asked. His other arm gripped her around the waist, keeping her back pressed against his front.

A soft whimper escaped her lips when he touched her there—the most private part of her.

He made a soft shushing sound. "Let me show you how much pleasure I can bring you."

And he did. He brought her more bliss than she had ever thought possible as his fingers stroked her. His other hand moved up to cup her breast again. Almost delirious from the sensations he coaxed from her, her head fell back against him. He pressed the side of his face against her cheek as he caressed her breast and continued his wicked movements below.

She couldn't think, could barely remember to breathe as pleasure overwhelmed her, just like he'd promised. And when it reached a point that she didn't think she'd be able to stand it any longer, her whole body seemed to convulse. His grip on her breast tightened briefly and he exhaled harshly, but the fingers of his other hand continued to move, prolonging the moment. Finally he stopped and released the fabric of her night rail so it fell around her, covering her once more.

They stood like that for at least a minute. His hand still on her breast, his cheek pressed against hers, and he wrapped his other arm around her waist, securing her to him as they both tried to regain control of their breathing.

As she came back to herself, she realized that he was still hard where he pressed into her back. Her thoughts were reeling... What had just happened? How had he affected her in such a way? And surely now he would take his own pleasure.

He released her and took a step back. She turned to face him, but he was already moving away. She stood, stunned, as he walked to the door that separated her room from his and crossed through it, closing the door behind him with almost exaggerated care.

JAMES HAD KNOWN his plan to introduce Sarah slowly to the physical side of marriage would prove difficult, but it had been harder than he'd imagined to keep from taking his new bride after she'd fallen apart so gloriously in his arms. He was hard and aching. It went against his nature to deny himself something he wanted so badly, especially when it was clear Sarah had been prepared to carry out her duty.

But if that day's events had shown him anything, it was that his new bride had not fully accepted their marriage. She'd been unfailingly polite when he'd courted her, but she hadn't encouraged his suit. Perhaps he should have given her more time to come to know him, but he'd known from the first time they met that he wanted her for his wife. He hadn't wanted to risk losing her to someone else. He couldn't say why, exactly, but she affected him in a way no other woman ever had.

He was well aware of his shortcomings and knew it would take time for Sarah to accept him fully. He wasn't classically handsome… certainly not as handsome as

Vaughan. His mouth twisted in distaste just thinking of the man.

Physically, James had more in common with dock-workers than his fellow members of the aristocracy, but he'd never wanted for female companionship. Those liaisons had been with women who were willing to engage in a little bed sport, but none of them had wanted to marry him. Not until he'd inherited his title. Then, overnight, he'd become a desirable catch.

But not for Sarah. She hadn't had a dowry and he hadn't cared. He had more money now than he could ever imagine spending. Still, she hadn't hidden her reluctance to marry him, and his conscience wouldn't allow him to forget that her parents had pressed her to accept him.

He paced the length of his room, unable to bear the thought of getting into his cold, lonely bed. He vowed silently that he would have Sarah. If her reaction to his touch that evening was any indication, it might even be as soon as the following night.

His palms itched with the need to touch her again, and his cock refused to go back down. It didn't help that he could still feel the warmth of her skin, could still smell her desire on his hands.

Cursing, he unbuttoned his trousers and set about giving himself some relief.

CHAPTER 4

*W*HEN SARAH WOKE the next morning, she was no less confused about the events that had taken place the previous evening. She'd expected Hathaway to climb over her and sate his desires within her body and had tried to prepare herself for that scenario. What happened instead had left her shaken. Instead of caring about his own pleasure, he'd thought only of her. And to her surprise, the desire he'd wrung from her had been more than she could ever have imagined.

And then he'd left.

She'd felt the evidence of his desire pressed against her back, so knew he'd wanted to go further. He hadn't, and she couldn't understand why. He'd wanted her, she was his wife and he could have had her, but instead he'd walked away.

But most confusing of all was the fact that she hadn't wanted him to leave. During those last few seconds, when she'd been certain he was about to remove her nightgown, she'd wanted him to do it.

It had occurred to her that in order to get through her wedding night she might have to pretend it was Robert who was touching her. In reality, her entire world had centered only on her husband. As she'd come apart in his arms, it was his face she saw, imagining the way he'd looked at her in the mirror. Everything about him was larger-than-life. How could any other man, even the memory of one she'd once loved, hope to compete when he was near? And for that reason, he posed a danger to her mental well-being.

Was he playing a game with her? In the light of day, she could see only one reason for his actions the previous night. He sought to unbalance her, to keep the upper hand in their relationship.

She wouldn't be able to avoid Hathaway forever, so she gathered her courage about her, imagining it was a cloak that safely shielded her, and made her way downstairs to the breakfast room.

He was already seated, and she had to endure having his eyes on her as she murmured a quiet greeting and moved to the sideboard where a wide variety of dishes was laid out. It was far more lavish than the breakfasts she'd had at home. Butterflies rioting in her belly, she helped herself to eggs and toast before returning to the table.

Self-consciousness threatened to overwhelm her as she gazed at her husband seated opposite her.

"How did you sleep last night, my lord?" She was

aiming for polite conversation but realized her mistake as soon as the words were out.

He gazed at her with mild amusement, one eyebrow quirked. "Horribly," he said. "But I trust your night was quite satisfactory."

At the reminder of the pleasure he had shown her, she glanced away, embarrassment causing her cheeks to heat.

"And don't you think it's time, Sarah, that you call me by my name?"

The way he uttered her name, as though he were relishing the sound of it on his tongue, did nothing to ease her embarrassment.

"Hathaway?" she asked, confused. Surely she'd already called him by his title. That was how she thought of him.

He shook his head. "No. James. I never expected to inherit, and I find I dislike having my wife call me by my uncle's title."

He'd mentioned a rift between him and the former viscount when they'd spoken in the gallery, and she could understand why the constant reminder of his uncle was unbearable.

She inclined her head in agreement. "I'll try... James."

His face lit with satisfaction and something else she couldn't name. When she found herself wanting to draw closer to him, she had to look away to break whatever spell he was casting over her.

She took a forkful of egg and had just managed to

swallow it when Hathaway—no, James—indicated that the footman leave the room. Then he brought up that which had been uppermost on her mind since he'd left the previous evening.

"We should talk about what happened last night."

Her fork clattered to the plate and she cast a furtive look at the door to see if the footman had overheard. She was relieved to find he was nowhere in sight. If he was waiting in the hallway, however, he might be able to hear their conversation.

She kept her voice low when she replied. "Must we?"

He appeared amused by her embarrassment. "Yes, we must. Especially since we are not legally married until the marriage is consummated."

She closed her eyes, hating that he wanted to talk about the physical side of their union. When she opened them again, his brows were drawn together in concern.

If they were going to talk about the previous night, she might as well take this opportunity to see if she could discover his true motivation for leaving her the night before. Had he been trying to manipulate her, or had he left for another reason?

"Why didn't you…" She waved a hand between them, asking without saying the actual words why he hadn't taken his own pleasure. And, as he'd rightly pointed out, made their marriage legal.

"Because I know you didn't want this marriage and you were afraid. I'm not the type of man to force myself on a woman, not even my own wife. But I did want to show you there was pleasure to be found in the marriage bed."

A new flood of heat crept into her cheeks as she remembered, again, just how he had touched her. "I think you already know that you succeeded in your goal."

He was silent for several moments as he stared intently at her. She could feel him examining her as though trying to read her thoughts. "Do you think you'll be afraid tonight?"

She looked away and tried to imagine him coming into her room after dinner. Remembering the anxiety she had felt as she waited for him last night, she expected some of that feeling to return. Instead, she had to face the truth. She was looking forward to seeing what else her husband could show her.

For a moment she considered putting him off but decided there was nothing to be gained. In fact, the opposite was true. By delaying the inevitable and denying the truth, she risked angering her husband and making things much worse between them.

She shook her head. "I don't believe so."

He closed his eyes briefly. "Thank God."

She could see, in that moment, just how much his consideration of her feelings had cost him. And she realized that perhaps their marriage wouldn't be the hardship she'd imagined.

∾

IT WAS NOT YET MIDDAY when Sarah was informed that her mother was waiting for her in the drawing room. Her mother hadn't said anything about planning to visit when she and her father had left the day before, and Sarah couldn't help but brace herself for bad news.

When she made her way to the drawing room, she found her mother unabashedly admiring the furnishings. The house had an inordinate amount of gold accents and gilded trim, and not just in the accessories or on the frames of the paintings. Sarah considered the decor more than a little ostentatious and wouldn't be surprised to learn that the arms of the settee were not merely covered with gold leaf but made from solid gold. The way James's uncle had thrown money about was almost shocking.

Her mother turned when Sarah entered and greeted her with a warm hug. Sarah exhaled in relief and lowered herself onto the settee, inviting her mother to join her.

"This is a surprise, Mama. I didn't expect you to visit quite so soon."

Her mother made a fluttering motion with her hand. "I know you're still on your honeymoon, but surely a mother can be excused for caring about her daughter's happiness."

Sarah bit back a sharp retort about how her mother hadn't seemed concerned about her happiness when she and her father had forced her to accept Lord Hathaway's proposal of marriage. Instead, she said, "I'm as well as can be expected."

Her mother pressed her lips together and looked away. "Was last night so terrible?"

Sarah could have kicked herself for her words. She'd consoled herself that in marrying Hathaway… no, James… and having him settle Papa's debts, she'd at least be able to lessen some of her mother's worries. And here she was adding to them.

"Last night was…" What could she say? That her wedding night had been wonderful, more amazing than she'd thought possible? That her new husband had been incredibly generous and had thought only of her pleasure? "He was gentle with me," she said finally. The words were inadequate, but she was reluctant to discuss the details of what had transpired between her and James. Especially since it was clear from her mother's warnings that the physical side of her own marriage was far from satisfying.

Her mother cast her eyes upward. "Thank heavens. I couldn't stop thinking about how you'd fare."

Sarah laid a hand over her mother's, which were clenched in her lap. "Can we talk about something else? I love you, Mama, but one conversation about what happens between a husband and a wife was already more than enough for me."

Her mother gave a small laugh, her relief obvious, and turned a hand over to squeeze Sarah's before releasing it. "I understand. It's not something I enjoy, but it is a burden all wives bear."

Trying hard not to think of her parents sharing similar intimacies to what she had experienced, Sarah changed the subject. "How is Papa today? I imagine he's quite satisfied with himself."

Her mother made a soft tsking sound at the peevish tone Sarah was unable to conceal. "He is happy, yes, but you can hardly expect him to feel otherwise. Your match was more than he could have hoped for."

"Because he gambled away my dowry?"

"Must we talk about this?" Her mother stiffened and looked away again.

What was the matter with her? Why must she insist on bringing up subjects that would only make her mother anxious again? Papa's selfishness meant that her mother was as much a victim of his excesses as she and her brother.

"I'm sorry, Mama. Please tell me, how is George? He almost didn't arrive in time for my wedding, and I barely spoke to him yesterday."

"You know your brother. He was anxious about missing school and is already on his way back to Eton. He left early this morning." Her mother lifted one shoulder in an attempt to appear indifferent, but Sarah could tell that her brother's haste to escape his family had hurt her. If Papa had celebrated her marriage last night in his usual manner—by imbibing just a little too much and becoming bitter and melancholy—she couldn't blame him. Now fifteen, at least her brother could escape their father's outbursts by spending as much time as possible at school.

"I always envied him, you know. That he was able to escape Papa's moods for most of the year."

A ghost of a smile touched her mother's lips, but it didn't reach her eyes. "I daresay he might say the same of you now."

Her mother's statement made Sarah sad beyond words. For her mother there would be no escape from her father's angry moods when he gambled and lost far more than they could afford. The one time Sarah had raised the subject directly with her mother, she'd replied that she would gladly take hurtful words over physical violence. Something in her mother's eyes had led her to believe that she'd experienced the latter, or at least been witness to it, but Sarah hadn't pursued the conversation. She was sure that made her weak, but she hadn't wanted to know.

"Enough of this grim subject," Sarah said. "Now that Papa's debts are settled, I'm sure he'll be content. Would you like me to show you the rest of the house?"

Her mother couldn't hide her hopeful expression even as she shook her head. "I fear I've already taken up too much of your time…"

Sarah waved her hand in dismissal of her mother's reservations. "Nonsense. Besides, it will help me to refresh my own memory. This house is so large I fear I've already forgotten much from the tour the house-keeper took me on yesterday." She stood and held her arm out to her mother. "Shall we?"

CHAPTER 5

To SAY THAT DINNER was a stilted affair would have been a vast understatement. It was just the two of them, and his new wife had informed the staff to serve their meal in the breakfast room instead of the much larger dining room.

In that moment, when he'd stood to welcome her as she entered the room, he realized just how much they had in common. As the only brother to the former Viscount Hathaway, there was no question that his father would be accepted by the *ton*. But his family almost never ventured out into society, and the formal trappings of that world—his world now—felt unnatural to him. He was more comfortable raising horses in the stables his father had founded than negotiating the ballroom, and he struggled with what to say and what was expected of him in this new life.

Given the modest means by which her family lived, Sarah's simple request to have their meal served in the smaller room spoke volumes as to her character. He'd expected his new wife to revel in the wealth that came with her new position. He had no doubt that she could hold her own in even the most imposing of dining rooms. The fact that she'd sought out comfort over formality gave him hope for their relationship.

The tension in the room was almost palpable, and James struggled for a way to ease it. From the way Sarah avoided his gaze as the first course was served, he knew she was thinking about their conversation that morning. He'd asked her if he could make love to her tonight and she had agreed.

He'd thought of little else all day.

He'd tried to distract himself, somehow managing to stay away from the house so he wouldn't drag Sarah up to his bedroom to make up for the wedding night he'd denied himself. He'd gone first to the dower house to visit his mother and sister. His mother tended toward self-sacrifice, and he wanted to ensure his family didn't want for anything. After leaving them, he'd headed to the stables.

Inheriting the viscountcy had affected his entire family. James's father had received only a modest inheritance that consisted of a small, unentailed property in Newmarket. He'd taken that inheritance and founded a stable that had gone on to become one of the best in all of England.

James had continued his father's legacy when the stables had passed down to him and his brother Edward. His passion for raising horses hadn't ended now that he was the viscount. For all his uncle's excesses, the stables at Hathaway Park were unexceptional, and James had only been able to bring a handful of horses with him to Northampton. But work was currently underway to construct new, larger stables. He hoped when his brother retired from the military that together they'd be able to expand the business.

Despite managing to fill the hours until it was time for dinner, it had been next to impossible to stop his thoughts from drifting to his wife and everything he wanted to do when he finally had her alone again. She probably wouldn't enjoy their first coupling, but he'd make it up to her in other ways.

He shifted in his seat as he began to grow hard. Again. He'd been half hard for most of the day.

So lost was he in thoughts of the coming night he almost didn't realize Sarah was speaking to him.

"Mrs. Phillips mentioned that you went to visit your mother and sister. They are more than welcome to stay here."

"Emily would like nothing better, but mother is finding her change in station a little overwhelming. I tried to convince her to move into the manor, but she prefers the smaller dower house. It reminds her of our former home."

Her brow furrowed, and she was silent for several seconds before saying, "I hope you're not saying that to spare my feelings. I imagine any mother would want more for her son than to marry the daughter of a man who'd gambled away everything that wasn't entailed."

Her words took him by surprise. He never imagined that she'd believe she wasn't good enough for him. The thought was laughable.

"To be completely honest, Uncle was horrible to us. The rest of us paid no attention to his snide comments about our branch of the family, but his belief that he was our superior in every way bothered my mother more than a little. I fear it has tainted her enjoyment of her new situation. She's here only as a show of support to me. If she had her preference, she'd be returning home." He scowled as he remembered just how much the old viscount had upset his mother.

"Well then, I'd say we're evenly matched. I know for a fact your uncle never approved of my family. I daresay he's turning over in his grave even as we speak."

The corners of his mouth lifted in amusement. His wife had wit and spirit. He liked that about her.

"To upsetting my uncle's plans," he said, raising a glass.

With a small laugh, she raised her own glass, and they shared an unexpected moment of quiet cama-raderie.

They fell into silence again as they finished their meal. Minutes ticked by and he could sense Sarah growing more tense. Much to his chagrin, he found himself considering if the best course of action would be to continue in the same vein as the previous evening. But he honestly didn't think he had it in him to show such restraint a second time, which meant he might just have to absent himself altogether after dinner.

When dessert was served and he had to endure watching his wife close her eyes as she enjoyed the syllabub, his control almost snapped. He barely restrained himself from taking her hand and leading her upstairs right then.

Finally, after what was surely an eternity, the meal was finished and the last plate whisked away. When Sarah looked at him, there was no missing the fact that her nerves were back in full force.

"I am at a loss as to what happens now," she said. "Normally my mother and I withdraw to the drawing room after dinner and I read while she sews. My brother joins us when he's home. On those rare occasions that he doesn't go to the tavern, my father buries himself in his study."

She licked her lips, and he was powerless to keep his eyes from following the motion of her small tongue as it flicked across her top lip. He almost groaned aloud.

"I don't suppose you wish to retire to your study now?"

He met her gaze, and reflected in her eyes he could see that she knew very well what he wanted. Relief filled him when he realized that while she might be nervous, he couldn't detect even a hint of the fear he'd seen the night before.

He pushed back his chair as he rose and held his hand out to her. She hesitated only a moment before placing her hand in his. He pulled her to her feet.

She tried to draw away, but he didn't release her.

"I'd like to retire now, but not to the study."

She swallowed and gave a small nod. "I'll ring for my maid and prepare for... bed."

He should let her go—it was the civilized, courteous thing to do—but he was incapable of letting her out of his sight. "I don't think you'll need her tonight."

She stared at him, uncomprehending, for several seconds. He could see the moment she realized his meaning when color swept into her cheeks. He released her hand then but held out his arm for her to take. He almost expected her to step away from him, but instead she took a deep breath and placed her hand on his arm.

A heady mixture of relief and desire filled him as he turned toward the door. She didn't lean against him. Their only point of contact was the touch of her hand, but his body vibrated with tension at her proximity. It seemed almost impossible that this was going to happen. That he'd finally have Sarah in his bed. When he'd first met her a scant few months before after taking up residence at the Hathaway family seat, he wasn't sure he'd ever see this day. And the fear in her eyes yesterday whenever they were alone together had only increased that doubt.

He was almost afraid to look at her as they made their way upstairs, afraid that if he did, he'd see that her fear had returned. But as long as he restrained himself, giving her time to remember what it had felt like to come apart in his arms, she would be his. He'd never lain with a chaste woman before, but he would be gentle. It might kill him, but he wouldn't push her until she was prepared to accept him.

He slowed when they reached the door of his bedroom but then moved past it to hers, reasoning that she would feel more comfortable in familiar surroundings. It would also help her to remember the pleasure he had already shown her in that room.

When they reached her door, she took her hand from his arm. He felt the loss keenly and almost snatched it back.

"Alice will wonder why I didn't ring for her," she said as she fumbled with the doorknob before finally opening the door.

Afraid she was about to leave him standing in the hallway, he pushed his way into the room behind her. "If she does, I'm sure one of the other servants will explain it to her."

She blushed, and he found himself aching to see that color spread over her chest again as it had the night before when he'd brought her to her peak. He closed the door before facing her again.

She swallowed, clearly nervous, but he knew he could make those nerves disappear. If there was one thing he'd learned over the years, it was how to please a woman.

"Are you afraid?" He didn't think she was, but he needed to be certain.

"No," she said with a shake of her head. "But I don't know what I'm supposed to do now."

He leaned toward her and spoke in a conspiratorial whisper. "Well, since I've deprived you of your maid this evening, you can consider me her replacement."

Taking her cue from him, she surveyed him from head to foot, paying particular attention to his hands before replying. "The buttons on my dress are quite small. I'm not sure you'll be able to manage them."

He smiled, relieved that she appeared to be softening to him. "I accept your challenge," he said, placing his hands on her shoulders and turning her away from him.

And a challenge it was. Halfway down the long row of buttons, he had to force himself to continue with what were probably the smallest buttons known to man. He tamped down on the temptation to yank apart the rest of the dress and send the buttons scattering.

When he finally reached the end, he spread the material apart and, without a word, began to unlace her corset. Her breathing quickened, and when he dropped a kiss onto her shoulder, he felt the tremor that ran through her body.

"I never imagined being undressed could be quite so stimulating," she said.

He lowered the dress from her shoulders. "You should feel free to press me into service whenever you'd like."

He released the dress and watched as it fell to the floor around her. When she stepped out of the pile of fabric, he pulled away her corset and cast it aside.

Like he had the night before, he pulled her body against his—her back to his front—and raised his hands to cover her breasts through her chemise. She released a soft sigh and dropped her head back against his shoulder, enjoying the way he was stroking her. Tearing himself from her side the previous evening had been one of the most difficult things he'd ever had to do, and he was glad he'd restrained himself, but tonight there would be no stopping.

He breathed against the side of her throat and felt another shiver of awareness go through her as he dropped a kiss there, then against her jaw and her cheek.

"Do you want me to continue?" His voice was rough and he knew the question was a gamble. He didn't think he'd be able to stop—the unspoken signals Sarah was giving him told him that she didn't want that either— but it was important to him that she realize she was a willing participant in their marriage. Her parents might have compelled her to marry him, but she did want him. Even if that want was only physical, he needed her to acknowledge it.

She made an inarticulate sound, but her eyes were still closed. He stilled his caresses and repeated the question. When she nodded in reply, he hesitated, considering whether he should press her for the words. He decided against it, knowing that he'd already risked too much by giving her the opportunity to say no. But before this night was over, he vowed that she'd have no doubt she craved his touch as much as he did hers.

He turned her to face him. When she gazed up at him, her warm brown eyes were slightly dazed. Lust, hot and swift, stole his voice. He lowered his head, determined to show her that she would not regret placing her trust in him.

He hadn't kissed her last night, and when she opened her mouth without prodding, he realized he wasn't the first man to kiss her this way. Jealousy speared through him, but he pushed it aside and dedicated himself to making her forget whoever had gone before him.

His need to take her was so great his hands were almost shaking. He pulled back to remove his tailcoat and tossed it onto a chair. Her eyes were riveted on him as he did so. He might not be conventionally handsome, but women had always appreciated his body. He sincerely hoped his wife would be one of those women. He was not unaccustomed to hard work, and it showed in his physique, but as a gently bred woman Sarah would be used to men who weren't quite so muscular.

He watched her carefully for any sign of fear as he undid the buttons of his waistcoat. Seeing none, he removed the garment, tossed it on top of his coat, and proceeded to untie his cravat.

Her eyes moved to the exposed skin at his throat before she looked away.

She started to turn, but he wouldn't let her shy away from him now.

He reached for her hand and stopped her. "Have you changed your mind?"

"No, my lord." She wet her lips before saying, "No, James."

He frowned and almost groaned at the gesture. "Then why are you running away?"

She searched for a reply and he waited, knowing it

was difficult for her to talk about their intimate life so openly.

"I thought… I was told…" She closed her eyes and took a deep breath before rushing on. "Isn't that what happens now? I lie on the bed and you… take your marital rights." As she reached the end of her statement, her voice was barely audible.

"I don't want a martyr, Sarah. I mean to show you that there can be great pleasure between a man and a woman."

Color bloomed on her skin, extending down beyond the edge of her chemise. It was with great difficulty that he kept his eyes on her face.

"I already know that. But tonight it is your turn."

"And you think that means you must be brave and suffer my touch while I seek my own pleasure?"

She raised a hand to rub the back of her neck. "I was told that was what to expect."

"By whom?"

If his wife had had the power to make herself disappear, he could tell she would have done so in that moment.

"My mother."

He winced as he tried to envision just how such a conversation would go. "I won't lie, the first time will probably be uncomfortable." He hoped it would only be that—he hated the idea of hurting her. "But I will do my best to make up for that initial pain."

She didn't appear convinced.

"Let's try this." Threading his fingers through hers, he led her to the bed.

He sat on the edge and pulled her into his lap. She inhaled deeply but didn't balk at the intimacy.

"For our first time together, I thought that you might prefer to take the lead."

Right now his wife was like one of his skittish colts who needed a gentle hand so he could gain its trust. That meant letting her control the pace to an extent.

When he saw her confusion, he had to hold back his smile. His wife truly was an innocent and the thought did nothing to stem his arousal. In fact, the opposite was true.

She was sitting primly on his lap, her body angled away from his. He pulled her closer, and when she settled against him, he nuzzled the side of her neck, inhaling deeply. She smelled of some flower he couldn't name, but the scent wasn't overwhelming. He kissed her neck and she melted against him with a soft sigh, gripping his upper arms. He didn't think it possible to get any harder, but the proof of her desire and the fact that she seemed to trust him made a heady aphrodisiac.

She pulled back and turned her face toward him, initiating a kiss. His heart soared as he allowed her to take her time. It wasn't long, however, until he was taking control, turning her soft exploration of his mouth into something deeper.

When she tugged his shirt from his trousers and burrowed her hands underneath the hem, he couldn't hold back his groan of pleasure.

"Am I doing this right?" she murmured against his mouth.

His hands tightened on her waist, and he lifted her to straddle his lap. Her chemise bunched at her hips, and her eyes widened with shock when he pulled her core against his hardness. Barely restraining a curse of impatience, he lifted his shirt up and off before tossing it onto the floor.

Somehow he remained still when she leaned back to look at him. She skimmed her hands up his arms to his shoulders and then trailed them down his chest.

"You're so hard," she said with wonder.

"And you"—he cupped her breasts in his hands —"are delightfully soft."

"I'm a little *too* soft."

"For which I am eternally grateful." He brushed his thumbs across her nipples and watched as they hardened against her chemise. "You're wearing far too much," he muttered as he lifted her chemise away. She was now naked in his arms, save for her stockings, and straddling his hips while he wore only his trousers. He wanted nothing more than to strip them off, but they served as a much-needed barrier to help him keep the pace slow.

She made a small sound of dismay, but her protest died when he brought her fully against him. Her breasts pillowing against his bare chest, he took her mouth again. He couldn't say who initiated the movement, but his hands gripped her hips, and she was rocking against his covered erection, soft mewling sounds coming from the back of her throat.

When she stiffened, he tore his mouth from hers and looked down at her impassioned face. Her eyes were closed, her face flushed, and her mouth rounded in surprise. He held her like that, tight against him, while he struggled not to embarrass himself.

She came to herself slowly, and when she opened her eyes she must have seen how much his restraint was costing him. "Show me what to do for you."

His voice thick, he managed to say, "Unbutton my trousers and take me out."

She didn't hesitate, and his heart beat a heavy rhythm in his chest. When she'd slipped the last button through its housing, she reached past his smalls and touched him. He covered her hand with his, showing her how to hold him, how he liked to be stroked. Knowing he wouldn't last much longer, he grasped her wrist after several seconds and pulled her hand away.

"Am I doing it wrong?" Her brows were drawn together in concern.

"You're perfect, but right now I need to be inside you."

He saw the brief flicker of fear in her eyes before she straightened her shoulders and nodded. He couldn't stop now—he only hoped this first time wouldn't be too painful for her.

He rose just enough to pull his trousers and small-clothes down before sitting back on the bed, enjoying the way she gripped his shoulders so he wouldn't unseat her. When he brought her womanhood against his bare erection, they moaned in unison.

He forced himself to slow down and enjoy the feel of her slick heat against him.

"I had no idea this would feel so good."

And with those words his hard-won control snapped. He gripped her hips and lifted her so the blunt edge of his manhood pressed against her opening.

"You need to take control," he managed to grind out.

Her eyes widened, but whatever reservations she'd had were clearly gone. "I don't know how."

He closed his eyes, struggling not to move. "Lower yourself onto me."

When she took her lower lip between her teeth, he hissed out a breath. Brow furled, she started to drop over him. Fortunately, her climax had prepared her body to accept him. After an initial moment of hesitation, she bore down on him and he slid in easily. She stiffened and lowered her head onto his shoulder, and he forced himself not to move.

He trailed his hands up and down her back. "All will be well now. The most difficult part is behind you."

"You're so big," she said, and he groaned.

"When you think you're ready, rise and then lower yourself onto me again."

She was still for what felt like an eternity before tentatively lifting herself. He was half afraid she would slide off him completely, but then she reversed and sank onto him. Her breath shuddered out, and he could tell she was surprised that this time there was no pain.

He helped her then, guiding her movements with his hands on her hips while he captured her little sounds of pleasure with his mouth.

He wasn't going to last long. He pressed a thumb against her, right above where they were joined, and she whimpered. Her movements were almost frantic now, mirroring his own desperation as they both reached for that peak. He reached it first and brought her hard against him. Harder than he'd intended. When she cried out, he feared he'd hurt her, but the telltale shudder of her body as she tightened around him told him otherwise.

He struggled to catch his breath, his relief profound that she had been with him the whole time. He fell onto his back and she followed, draping herself over him.

They lay like that, their bodies still entwined, for several minutes. When he felt himself begin to harden again, he knew he had to return to his own bedroom. Sarah would be too sore to enjoy a second round of lovemaking, and he didn't trust himself not to press the issue.

Sarah had already fallen asleep, so he shifted slowly, careful not to wake her as he rolled her away from him. Every part of him screamed in protest when he stood, covered her with the blankets, and returned to his room and his cold bed.

CHAPTER 6

*S*ARAH WOULD HAVE THOUGHT it impossible that a man she barely knew, and for whom she had no romantic feelings, could bring her pleasure in the marriage bed. Yet that is exactly what had happened and she was at a loss to understand why.

After the intimacies they'd shared, she wasn't sure she'd be able to face James in the morning. She'd been told that her husband would take the lead in consummating their marriage and had thought all she'd have to do was lie back, endure, and pray it would soon be over. She should have realized James Hathaway wouldn't be content to behave in the expected manner. He had actually allowed her to take charge, and in the heat of passion, she'd done so with great enthusiasm.

He'd unbalanced her so thoroughly that she'd woken several times during the night from heated dreams of James making love to her over and over. So intense were those dreams that she could almost feel the weight of his hands on her. She'd been disappointed when he left her and chided herself for that sentimentality. Had she expected him to stay the whole night? There was a reason, after all, that married couples kept separate bedrooms.

She had to live now with the knowledge that her husband had firmly taken the upper hand in their marriage. She might have been innocent before marrying James Hathaway, but she wasn't a fool. It was obvious he was very experienced. She was woefully out of her depth and couldn't hope to have the same hold over her husband that he had gained over her.

It took her longer than normal to dress before venturing downstairs for breakfast, but her nerves instantly calmed when she learned that James had already eaten and gone out to meet with the builders for the new stables he was having constructed. She hated the fact that she was behaving like a coward, but she desperately needed time away from her husband if she hoped to maintain her composure in his presence.

She ate quickly, deciding she would get to know her husband's family that day. She'd been completely over-whelmed on the day of her wedding, most of her thoughts centering on how she would survive what she'd thought would be the ordeal of her wedding night. She'd concentrated mainly on smiling, trying to appear the happy bride, and hadn't spoken to James's mother or sister beyond their formal introductions. That would change today since his family was now hers.

After breakfast, she penned a note informing them that she planned to visit and arranged for a footman to deliver it. It was already midmorning, but she wanted to wait for a reply before descending on them. Perhaps one day they'd grow close enough that such formalities wouldn't be required, but until that happened she didn't want to presume on the relationship.

It was a cool morning, so she donned a cloak and sturdy walking shoes before venturing outside to explore the gardens as she waited for the footman to return. They were, of course, as formal and rigid in design as the former viscount. From what she knew of the viscount's widow, she seemed very friendly, so Sarah could only imagine that she hadn't been given leave to show any of her personality in either the house's furnishings or the garden.

As she walked amid the immaculately trimmed hedges, she wondered if she'd be allowed to make any changes. Excitement filled her at the thought. Perhaps James would allow her to curb some of the excesses in the house. The furnishings were unquestionably beautiful, but the formality of the decor made it difficult to feel truly at home.

She was mentally redesigning the drawing room—starting with the removal of the impractical gold settee that seemed designed to be admired rather than used—when the footman returned. Instead of the note she'd expected, the footman informed her that James's mother would be happy to receive her at any time.

The dower house was only a mile from the manor, a

distance she covered quickly on foot. Upon arriving, Sarah was ushered inside and shown into the drawing room where James's mother and sister were already waiting for her.

She could see immediately why her new mother-in-law preferred to live here rather than stay at the manor house with her son. The house was considerably smaller, but what it lacked in size, it made up for in warmth. Instead of delicate, ornate chairs that looked as though they would collapse under a person's weight, the furniture was made from deep mahogany and upholstered in rich green fabric. And the walls—she'd only seen the entryway and the drawing room, but there was actual color on the walls. Whereas the manor was furnished to impress visitors with the owner's wealth, this house was designed to be welcoming and warm. Given the choice, Sarah thought she'd prefer to live here as well.

James's mother was a petite woman, and it was difficult to believe that her husband had come from such a small person. Given his height and the breadth of his shoulders, she imagined that he took after his father in appearance. Mrs. Hathaway—who asked that Sarah not refer to her as "my lady" or "Lady Hathaway" as it made her uncomfortable, having only earned the title when her son inherited—couldn't be older than fifty. Gray streaked her dark hair, but she was still a beautiful woman. That beauty was reflected in her daughter, Emily.

Mrs. Hathaway was a quiet woman, but Sarah's

sister-in-law more than made up for her mother's reserve.

"I'm so happy you decided to visit," Emily said, linking her arm through Sarah's and leading her to the overstuffed settee. "I wanted to visit, but Mama said it was too soon. That you and James needed time alone together."

Sarah's thoughts immediately went to the things she and her husband had done the previous evening, and she felt the telltale heat of embarrassment color her cheeks. A quick glance at Mrs. Hathaway, who was attempting to hide her amusement, was sufficient to tell her that James's mother knew exactly what she was thinking.

"I've always wanted a sister," Emily said, oblivious to the knowing look that had passed between the two other women. "It's dreadfully dull having two older brothers. Though, with Edward gone, I will admit that I miss him. At least we still have James… and it was so kind of you to allow us to live here. I'd hoped to stay in the main house—it's very grand, is it not?—but Mama wanted to stay here. Not that I don't like this house. It's very pretty too."

Sarah stared at Emily, amused and charmed by her enthusiasm. "Goodness, I can see now why James is a man of few words. After you were born, he probably rarely had the opportunity to speak!"

As soon as the words were out, she feared Emily would take them the wrong way, but the young woman's breathless laugh told her she was not so easily offended.

Mrs. Hathaway took advantage of the break in Emily's chatter to speak. "Perhaps you should give Sarah the opportunity to tell us why she is here."

Emily waved an impatient hand. "Sarah is family now. We needn't stand on ceremony with her."

It was clear to Sarah that James's mother was not yet comfortable in her presence, but the woman couldn't find a way to repeat her rebuke without appearing impolite.

Sarah rushed to reassure her. "James is overlooking the plans for the construction of the new stables, so I thought today would be a good time for us to become better acquainted." She turned then to face Emily. "You already know I only have one brother, and I, too, have always longed for a sister. I think we will get on quite well. I suspect you wouldn't have it any other way," she said with her own laugh.

"See, Mama? I told you that James had chosen well."

Mrs. Hathaway shook her head in defeat, but the relaxed slope of her shoulders told Sarah that her words had put the woman at ease.

As they exchanged pleasantries, Sarah found it almost impossible to keep up with Emily's effusiveness, and she was happy to find that her original hope was proving to be true. Despite the fact that Emily was only sixteen—six years younger than Sarah—it was already clear to her that they would become close. It was impossible not to be captivated by Emily's guileless charm.

Mrs. Hathaway, on the other hand, was harder to draw out, but her initial reticence at the beginning of Sarah's visit seemed to have disappeared.

The soft chime of the clock over the mantel told her that almost an hour had passed. Content with the way the morning had gone, she stood to take her leave, but not before inviting James's mother and sister to join them for dinner that evening.

Emily's eyes lit up at the invitation, and she turned to her mother. "Can we go? Sarah wouldn't have invited us if she felt we'd be an imposition."

Mrs. Hathaway turned her eyes skyward for a second before letting out a soft sigh. When she met Sarah's gaze, however, it was amusement Sarah saw in her eyes.

"Thank you. As Emily has made clear, we would love to join you."

Emily must have been afraid that any further show of eagerness on her part might cause her mother to change her mind, for she said nothing more about the invitation, but Sarah could see her enthusiasm bubbling just below the surface. Her new sister-in-law might be able to hold still when the need arose, but she couldn't disguise the excitement dancing in her eyes.

Sarah was smiling when she left the dower house. She liked James's family very much, and it was clear that she was already beginning to like her husband as well. Perhaps too much. He still overwhelmed her, but he'd been nothing but kind to her so far. How was it possible that he was so much larger-than-life when his family was so down-to-earth?

She was starting to question whether she'd be able to keep her emotions from becoming involved with respect to her new husband, and that thought scared her to death.

CHAPTER 7

December 1812

ITH THE ASSISTANCE of the efficient Mrs. Phillips, Sarah acquainted herself with the running of Hathaway Park over the next few weeks. She still lost her way on occasion when she decided to venture into an unfamiliar part of the house, but those instances were finally occurring less frequently.

All too soon it was mid-December. Every year as Christmas approached, the Vaughans hosted a party. Some years, when the snow was heavy, only the families that lived closest to their estate attended. The Mapletons were included in that group. But since they'd yet to see any snow that year, Sarah knew that every family within a few hours' drive would be present.

As much as she'd wanted to, Sarah didn't protest when James mentioned receiving their invitation. As the new Viscount Hathaway, it was important that he become further acquainted with the families in the area, many of whom he hadn't seen since the wedding day. She only hoped she'd be able to avoid Robert Vaughan, the man she'd once thought she would marry.

The carriage ride took just over an hour, but that hour flew by thanks to Emily's excited chatter. Since her sister-in-law wouldn't be out for another two years, this would be the largest social event Emily had ever attended. Her enthusiasm helped ease the dread Sarah felt about the evening ahead.

Even James's normally reserved mother seemed to be looking forward to the evening. Her husband's demeanor, on the other hand, could only be described as stoic. He hadn't said as much to her, but she suspected he wasn't yet comfortable with his new title.

A small part of her wondered if some of his unease stemmed from the knowledge that she'd once had an understanding with Robert. But if James had learned of their former courtship, he hadn't mentioned it to her.

As the carriage drew nearer to the Vaughans' estate, Sarah couldn't stop thinking about the Christmas party the previous year, when she'd expected that this year she and Robert would either be betrothed or already married. She expected that memory to cause her pain. Instead, she was surprised to find that her grief at having lost the man she loved and being forced to marry someone she barely knew was no longer as acute as it had once been. She could only attribute that to her new husband. She didn't love James—after Robert's casual dismissal of her feelings, she would never again give a man that much power to hurt her—but she appreciated the fact that he went out of his way to ensure she would have no cause to fear him.

In fact, the opposite was true. She never would have thought it possible, but she found herself looking forward to their nightly lovemaking sessions. Her thoughts drifted to the previous night and, without realizing it, her eyes came to rest on James, who was seated opposite her.

He met her gaze, and she could tell he was either remembering last night as well or thinking about what would happen later in the evening. Her stomach dipped at the fire in his eyes, and a corresponding heat began to spread through her. They stared at each other for several long moments before she tore her gaze away. A quick glance at their companions assured her they hadn't noticed that James had the power to fluster her with merely a look.

The moon was out and the night clear, so she turned to stare at the bleak scenery outside the carriage window, thinking about how pretty it would look when the snow began to fall. She murmured responses to Emily's inquiries when they were required as she struggled to maintain her composure.

It was impossible to keep her thoughts from centering on the first month of her marriage. James had visited her every night, initiating her into a world of pleasure she'd never expected to experience with him. He was always gentle with her, ensuring she found pleasure before he returned to his own bedroom. But she suspected that he was holding back.

Their marriage was still so new and her husband still an unknown quantity. He was so big, so overwhelming. The fact that he seemed to hold himself so tightly leashed made her anxious about the day he finally lost that control. She'd seen all too well how her own father could change from one moment to the next, especially when he'd been drinking. The slightest transgression could change him from the kind country squire most people thought him to be to a man filled with rage and bitterness. He never physically hurt them, something for which her mother informed her and George that they should all be grateful, but that didn't change the fact that his words could cut as deep as a knife.

Much as she wanted to believe that her own marriage was vastly different from that of her parents, she went through her days feeling as though she were in limbo. On the surface, things were pleasant and certainly more than she could have hoped for, especially after her own dashed hopes with respect to Robert. But her husband was being far too circumspect in his treatment of her. She couldn't shake the feeling that the emotions bubbling beneath the surface would one day break free. She only hoped that when they did, they would be the gentle popping of bubbles reaching the surface when a kettle began to simmer and not the violent explosions that burst forth during a full boil.

Until that happened, she could only take comfort in witnessing how he treated his family. She'd watched

James with his mother and sister, when he didn't have that air of caution that was so evident when he interacted with her, and she had yet to see any evidence of a temper. But she also hadn't seen him when he was in his cups. Would his personality change then, like her father's did?

While her feelings toward her husband were conflicted, the same couldn't be said about her relationship with his mother and sister. After her initial wariness, Mrs. Hathaway had warmed to her, no longer seeming to fear that she would say something wrong or make a blunder. And Emily... in the short time Sarah had known her, Emily had become like a sister.

Since James was occupied with overseeing the planned expansion to the stables—hoping to make considerable progress before it got too cold or began to snow—and becoming acquainted with the running of an estate as large as the one he'd inherited, she was left to her own devices most days. Meeting with the housekeeper to go over the meals and the running of the household didn't take that much time out of her day. Sarah loved to draw, spending hours working on pencil sketches and watercolors. And Emily had taken to visiting her almost daily, but she only stayed for dinner twice a week on the evenings when her mother joined them.

When their carriage pulled to a stop before the Vaughan estate, James didn't wait for a footman to open the door. He leaped down from the carriage and turned, holding out a hand to assist the others.

She couldn't avoid the knowing look in his eyes when she placed her hand in his. The way his eyes traveled over her figure caused heat to rise in her cheeks again. She was wearing a cloak, but she knew him well enough to know he was already envisioning divesting her of the gown she wore beneath it.

"Behave," she whispered. She needn't have wasted her breath, for instead of being chastised, he lifted the corner of his mouth in a knowing smile that made her insides tingle before he released her hand and turned to assist his mother and sister.

While no longer painful, entering the house she knew almost as well as the one in which she'd been raised—and which she'd expected to one day become her home—made her more than a little uncomfortable. Her family and the Vaughans had once been very close, and she couldn't remember a time when she hadn't known Robert. But after he'd told her that her father was too steeped in debt to make a marriage between them possible, she'd never expected to cross this house's threshold again.

She held her breath as she did so now, taking comfort from James's solid presence at her side. She must have squeezed his arm because he looked down at her, one brow raised in question.

Before she could manufacture an excuse for her nerves, Emily claimed his other arm. "I'm so excited," she said with a smile that fairly beamed. Sarah wouldn't have been surprised if her sister-in-law started bouncing on her toes.

"The house looks lovely," Sarah said, acutely aware that James was watching her closely. And it did. As always, the Vaughans had spared no detail in decorating the house for the holiday.

While the butler took their outer garments, enlisting the aid of a footman, she took in the familiar home. Greenery spilled from containers that lined the entrance, and boughs were wrapped around the stair rail. Sarah didn't miss the mistletoe that hung from the doorways.

"Is that... It is, isn't it? That's mistletoe," Emily exclaimed, gazing up at the archway they were about to pass under.

Sarah could have kissed her sister-in-law at that moment, for her exclamation was enough to draw her husband's attention away from her.

"If anyone even contemplates kissing you, they'll live to regret it." James's tone was light, but Sarah could tell he spoke in earnest.

Emily frowned at her brother. "Who would I want to kiss? I don't even know anyone." She turned to look at Sarah. "How well do you know the Vaughans? Am I correct that your parents don't live far from here? You must know them well."

And there it was, out in the open—the question she'd been hoping to avoid. "My parents are friends with Mr. and Mrs. Vaughan. We've been coming to their Christmas party for as long as I can remember." She didn't dare meet James's eyes as she replied. He was far too perceptive, and she feared he'd sense that she wasn't being entirely truthful.

They passed under the archway, following the butler to the small ballroom at the back of the house. It was a modest-sized room, but Sarah knew how proud Mrs. Vaughan was that their house was large enough to have a ballroom. Sarah's parents couldn't boast as much despite the fact that her father was a baronet.

When the butler announced their arrival, every eye in the room turned their way. The room was full to overflowing. She couldn't remember there ever being so many guests in previous years and realized most of the partygoers must be here to see the new viscount and viscountess.

She shook off her slight unease at being the center of so much attention as they greeted Mr. and Mrs. Vaughan. Robert was there as well. Fortunately, he was off to one side, speaking to one of their neighbors. It was bad enough having to see him at all, but she wouldn't have been able to bear having to greet him under the watchful eyes of his parents.

"We're honored that you chose to attend," Mrs. Vaughan said. "Your uncle never had time... I'm sure he was very busy."

Sarah glanced at her husband, wondering what he was thinking as he murmured a few words in greeting and turned the subject to the unseasonably warm weather. Everyone knew that his uncle had thought himself above everyone there.

Mrs. Vaughan turned to her next. "We are so pleased to see you again, Sarah. It was a pleasant surprise to receive the invitation to your wedding."

Sarah smiled, hoping that her unease wasn't evident. "I'm glad you and Mr. Vaughan were able to attend."

The fact that she hadn't mentioned Robert didn't go unnoticed. The look of compassion on Mrs. Vaughan's face almost killed her, and she had a frantic moment of worry that her husband would realize the other woman was trying to communicate her sympathy. She might not love James, but she did respect him, and she wouldn't allow anyone to disparage him. Not like she had on their wedding day when he'd overheard one of her cousins extending sympathy on her marriage.

She was prevented from responding when the butler announced another arrival and James drew them away. Her husband was almost immediately swept away by a group of men eager for the opportunity to befriend the new Viscount Hathaway.

As she watched James walk away, she couldn't help but compare him to Robert, struck anew by their differences. James was tall, broad across the chest and shoulders and dark haired, while Robert was the complete opposite in nearly every way. The only thing they had in common was their height, but James was still a few inches taller.

Robert was more like the old viscount in appearance —fair-haired and slim. She'd once thought him the most handsome man of her acquaintance, but somehow his appeal had dimmed. When she looked at him now, the yearning she'd expected to feel was absent. She could only attribute it to the fact that her eyes had been opened as to his selfishness in the most blunt manner possible when he'd casually dismissed her feelings for him because of her lack of fortune.

She refused to believe there was another reason for her lack of emotion toward the man she'd once expected to wed.

Sarah introduced Emily and Mrs. Hathaway to several of their neighbors. Emily was in her element, unable to hide her enthusiasm at attending her first ball, and Mrs. Hathaway seemed to overcome her shyness with every person who greeted her warmly. But Sarah didn't miss the way her mother-in-law frowned whenever she happened to glance at their hostess, confirming that she had caught the other woman's slight toward James.

THE MOMENT he entered the ballroom, awareness that he didn't belong settled over James. He didn't look like a typical gentleman, being both taller and broader than any other man in attendance. He could hide his work-roughened hands inside the gloves he wore, but could do nothing to conceal the fact that he'd spent countless hours toiling under the sun.

The awareness that everyone was sneaking glances at him, judging him, reminded him, yet again, that his uncle had thought him unworthy of inheriting his title. James did his best to push those negative thoughts to the back of his mind where they usually resided, but as he was discovering more and more lately, those doubts about his suitability were no longer content to remain buried.

It didn't help that the Vaughans and many of the other guests seemed to be going out of their way to impress him. He wasn't sure what they expected from him. He couldn't tell if they believed that he thought himself better than them. Certainly his uncle had held that belief, and from everything James had learned, the former viscount had rarely interacted with his neighbors. Or perhaps they saw through his facade, seeing him for the ordinary man he was, and were waiting for him to embarrass himself.

Whatever the case, he couldn't shake the sensation that he was on display. It certainly wouldn't be an exaggeration to say that every man present had approached him and attempted to monopolize his time.

The dull throbbing of his jaw made him aware that he was clenching his teeth, and he had to force himself yet again to relax. He wanted nothing more than to walk away from the incredibly dull duo that was bragging about improvements they'd recently made to their respective estates, each one trying to outdo the other by going on about how much money they had spent. He tried to feign interest even as he became aware that the small group of musicians playing in one corner of the room was coming to the end of yet another set. He'd made it a point to see if Sarah was dancing, but so far she'd remained by his mother's and sister's side. He'd hoped to dance with her that evening, to show her that she hadn't married someone who was completely without manners.

When the dinner bell rang, he made good his escape. He inclined his head to the two men and turned to the right, where he'd last seen Sarah. But before he could start toward her, Mrs. Vaughan commanded his attention. It took him a moment to realize that as the highest-ranked guest present, he would be seated next to her during dinner. That was just another of the annoyances that came with inheriting his title—he could no longer choose who he sat next to at dinner.

Instead of the curse that sprang to his lips, he greeted the older woman with a smile and offered her his arm. Again, he chafed under the realization that many of the guests were watching them as they made their way from the room.

When everyone was finally settled around the long dining table, he wasn't surprised to see that his wife was seated at the far end of the table, next to their host. Annoyance flared, however, when he saw that Robert Vaughan sat on her other side.

He found it almost impossible to keep his attention from drifting to the pair and was only half listening to what their hostess was saying. But finally her words penetrated his preoccupation.

"They make such a lovely pair, don't you agree?" He glanced at Mrs. Vaughan then and saw that she, too, was looking at Sarah and her son. "We were so disappointed that things didn't work out between them.

Between you and me, I'm afraid that Robert broke Sarah's heart."

Her voice faltered when he swung his gaze back to the older woman, incredulity mixing with more than a hint of anger. Surely she didn't think it polite dinner conversation to tell someone that their wife was in love with another man.

"But of course," she rushed to add, "everything worked out in your favor."

He couldn't tell if she was referring to her son's thwarted relationship with Sarah or if she also included how much James had gained after his uncle's death. In the end, it didn't matter. He decided then and there that his uncle had the right idea in avoiding his neighbors. He wouldn't go so far as to ignore everyone, but he couldn't foresee a time when he would cross over the Vaughans' threshold again.

For now he chose to remain and act as though he wasn't the brute many no doubt thought him to be. While he wanted nothing more than to drag Sarah away from the slim young man who seemed intent on capturing his wife's attention, he wouldn't embarrass her by making a spectacle of himself.

But that didn't mean his temper wasn't boiling beneath the surface. He took a small measure of satisfaction in turning away from their hostess, focusing his attention on the older woman seated at his other side. Mrs. Vaughan's soft sound of distress when he continued to ignore her soothed his pride only a tiny fraction because he couldn't turn a blind eye to what was happening at the other end of the table.

The younger Vaughan made a great deal of effort at first to engage Sarah in conversation, but his wife demurred and seemed to concentrate on her food. James couldn't tell if she was trying to dissuade Vaughan from conversation or attempting to be coy.

James had just managed to convince himself that his wife didn't want the other man's attention when he saw her eyes narrow at the way Robert was speaking to Emily, who was seated next to them. Sarah continued to watch Robert carefully as he spoke to her sister-in-law, and James almost snapped the stem of the glass he raised to his lips.

He realized that he didn't know his wife very well... aside from the fact that she'd been vehemently against marrying him of course. It was true that she came alive in his arms at night, but their relationship outside the bedroom could only be considered cordial at best. Jealousy churned in his gut as he was presented with the very real possibility that his wife was still in love with another man.

CHAPTER 8

*S*UPPER HAD BEEN more uncomfortable than she'd feared. Sarah couldn't imagine what Robert's mother had been thinking to seat them together. He'd been charming and courteous to both her and Emily, which had made her more than a little uncomfortable. She was grateful, however, that Robert had acted as though they were merely acquaintances, treating her no differently than he did Emily.

But every time she'd spotted James looking their way, she couldn't help but feel a twinge of guilt. Guilt for doing nothing more than attempting to enjoy her meal. She hadn't been able to eat more than a few bites of every course. Mrs. Vaughan had outdone herself with the sheer amount of food they'd served, and it had all been delicious. But at some point near the start of the meal, she'd become aware of the fact that James was angry. She'd spent the remainder of the meal with her stomach in knots.

Now, standing at the side of the ballroom again with Mrs. Hathaway, she cringed as Robert approached. She sent up a silent prayer that he wouldn't invite her to dance.

He stopped before them and executed a deep bow. It took everything in her power not to roll her eyes when he straightened and smiled at them. It was always thus, though it had never bothered her before now. Robert was so used to everyone thinking the sun rose and set on his shoulders that he took it as his due that he had merely to smile at someone and they would fall at his feet.

He turned to Mrs. Hathaway, making a remark about the weather and asking her if she was enjoying the evening. In truth, Sarah was barely paying attention to him. Her eyes followed her husband as a group of men that included her father drew him away from the room. She knew her parent well, and since the Vaughans normally set up a card room, she imagined they'd enticed him to join them in a game.

She wasn't worried about James. From everything she'd learned, he could well afford to play and not worry about going into debt. And truthfully, from the successful horse-breeding business he'd run before inheriting, she imagined he was good with money and would never wager more than he could afford to lose.

Her father, however, was another matter. He'd already been on the verge of losing everything before bartering away her hand in marriage. Was he hoping that James would continue to finance his penchant for wagering money he didn't have?

She knew James had paid all her father's gambling debts and that he hadn't cared that she'd come to the marriage with no dowry. She hadn't seen the actual marriage contract, however. How much money had James given her father? And how much more would he continue to give him?

She struggled with the unease that settled in the pit of her stomach. In truth, it wasn't just the money that concerned her. Her father always drank liberally when he played, and if he lost, it would put him in a foul mood. A mood that would have him heaping verbal abuse on her mother all the way home.

Robert caught her attention again when he said, "I know your daughter isn't out yet. This is just a small Christmas celebration, not even a country ball really. But I couldn't help being charmed by Miss Hathaway's enthusiasm over supper. I thought she might like to join me for the next dance."

"Emily is only sixteen," Sarah said.

Robert's smile remained in place as he glanced at her before turning his attention back to Mrs. Hathaway, but she hadn't missed the way his jaw tightened. *Good, let him be annoyed*, she thought.

Emily turned a look of pleading on her mother.

"I don't see the harm," Mrs. Hathaway said with a smile.

Sarah could only look at her in surprise. No harm?

James would be angry. He was no longer in the room, however. Perhaps he wouldn't learn of Emily's dance with Robert. Almost as soon as that thought occurred to her, Sarah realized that Emily wouldn't be able to stop talking about her first dance. James would definitely find out about it.

Despite her misgivings, she said not a word as Robert smiled down at Emily and held out his arm. Emily didn't hesitate to take it, and Sarah was struck by just how pretty her sister-in-law looked tonight. Her stomach tightened further when Robert had the temerity to wink at her before leading Emily out.

"James won't be happy," Sarah said when the pair was no longer within hearing range. She wished he were here now to put a stop to what was happening. In that moment, she realized that she was also disappointed her husband hadn't stayed in the ballroom and asked her to dance.

Mrs. Hathaway made a small noise of impatience. "James is far too protective. Emily isn't the only girl not yet out who is dancing."

Her mother-in-law was correct of course. In fact, it didn't seem all that long ago when Sarah used to look forward to the Vaughans' annual Christmas gathering for just that reason.

The opening strains of a quadrille began to play, and she watched as Robert bowed to his partner. Emily's smile widened as she curtsied, and it occurred to Sarah to wonder just how large Emily's dowry would be.

Worse, she realized Robert might be hoping to ensnare the girl's interest since it was almost certain Emily would come to her future marriage with a sizable settlement.

Her mother approached them then, and while Sarah managed to keep track of the conversation between her mother and Mrs. Hathaway, her gaze kept drifting back to Emily and Robert. The young woman moved with a grace that shouldn't have surprised Sarah. It might have been Emily's first ball, but it was clear she had practiced her dancing. What concerned Sarah most about their dance, however, was the way Emily was looking at Robert. She feared that James's sister was in danger of developing feelings for him.

"Sarah, you're distracted," her mother said, peering around Mrs. Hathaway to see what her daughter was looking at. When she spied Robert and Emily, she released a soft "Oh dear."

Mrs. Hathaway frowned. "What is the matter? I know Emily is still too young for a proper ball, but since we are informal here and there are others her age dancing, I didn't see the harm in allowing her the liberty."

Her mother looked at her, and Sarah gave a small shake of her head. The very last thing she needed was to have her mother discussing her past *disappointment*—how she hated that word—with James's mother.

"It is nothing. I was merely curious. Is there..." Her mother hesitated, and Sarah braced herself, unsure if her mother would reveal her past connection to Robert. "Is there something more between Emily and Robert?"

Mrs. Hathaway's brows lifted at the question. "Of course not. Why would you think there was?"

"No reason," her mother said before glancing over the other woman's shoulder. "Oh, I see Mrs. Henderson. If you'll excuse me, I must speak to her."

After watching Sarah's mother scurry away, Mrs. Hathaway turned to her. "Is there something I should know?"

Sarah waged an inner debate and, in the end, decided that she couldn't lie to the woman. But that didn't mean she'd tell her the entire truth. She certainly wouldn't tell her that Robert had broken her heart. "At one time, people thought that Robert and I would make a match. But of course that never happened."

She'd meant to keep her words light, but the other woman must have detected the hint of anger she'd been unable to disguise.

"I see," she said simply.

If she wanted to know more, she was too polite to ask, something for which Sarah was more than a little grateful. The last thing she wanted to discuss with her current mother-in-law was her former feelings for Robert Vaughan. Fortunately, she didn't have to search for a way to change the subject. Her husband's attendance was the most exciting thing to happen at the Vaughans' Christmas ball in years, and that meant the company of his wife and mother would be sought out by all their neighbors.

When the current set came to an end and the pair she'd been unable to keep herself from watching returned, Emily's cheeks were flushed in a most becoming fashion. She kept glancing up at Robert with something akin to rapt adoration on her face. The way he looked down at Emily left Sarah with no doubt that he was doing everything in his power to encourage that feeling. It took a great deal of effort on Sarah's part to keep from frowning.

Instead of excusing himself, Robert stayed with their group, engaging her companions in light banter. With each passing minute, Sarah realized that her suspicions about his intentions toward Emily hadn't been an over-reaction on her part.

"I'm quite thirsty," Sarah said when she couldn't stand it any longer. She had to put an end to Robert's schemes. "Would you mind fetching a drink for me?"

Robert hesitated only a moment, but after meeting her gaze, he excused himself with the promise that he'd return shortly. They'd done that in past years when they'd wanted to spend some time together, inventing an excuse to meet for a few minutes of privacy. She watched his progress, and when she saw him slip from the ballroom, she knew he'd understood her intent.

The last thing she wanted was another secret meeting with him, but it couldn't be helped. She had to speak to him in private, convince him to turn his atten-tion elsewhere. Emily was still two years away from coming out, and she could say with certainty that her husband wouldn't welcome any advances from potential suitors until that time.

She made a vague excuse to Emily and Mrs. Hathaway, whose attention had already been ensnared by another of their eager neighbors. As she slipped from the room, it only then occurred to her that it was possible Robert had misconstrued her intention. She quickly shook off that thought. Even if she were the kind of woman to betray her husband, Robert knew her well enough to realize that her pride would never allow her to make a fool of herself over any man. Especially not one who had so little regard for her feelings.

She moved past two rooms, grateful that she didn't have to pass the card room on her way to the library. Relief swept through her when she reached her destination without encountering anyone. She slipped into the room and closed the door behind her.

The lighting in the library was much dimmer than it had been during their meetings in past years, a solitary lamp on a low table providing the only illumination. She realized in that moment that Robert had made a point to prepare the room ahead of time for one of their Christmas interludes. Clearly, he was hoping that tonight they would go much further than whispered words and a few kisses.

She turned when he moved out of the shadows to her right.

"This is a pleasant surprise," he said, his smile smug as he moved far too close for her comfort.

She took a step back and his smile faltered.

"I'm here only because I need to speak to you."

His easy smile returned, and she found herself

wanting to wipe it from his face. She licked her lips as she tried to think about how best to approach the subject without coming out and accusing him of being a fortune hunter.

"I need to speak to you about Emily. She is still very young and impressionable."

"She's not any younger than you and I were when we first kissed."

She winced at the reminder. "And look at how well that ended."

He didn't try to hide his amusement. "I understand your disappointment. And I must say, I find your display of jealousy heartening."

"I'm not jealous," she said immediately. It was the truth—her only concern was for Emily—but she could tell he didn't believe her. She shrugged off her annoyance. After all, it didn't really matter what he believed. All that mattered was that he not take advantage of James's sister. "Just promise me that you won't encourage Emily. I don't want to see her hurt."

His mouth turned down at that, his eyes narrowing. "That's hardly fair, Sarah. You know very well I couldn't marry you when I learned your family was on the brink of financial ruin. But you've done very well for yourself. I don't understand why you'd deny me the same opportunity."

"This isn't about me or what happened between us in the past. My only motivation in speaking to you now is to ensure that you don't hurt Emily."

He continued on as though she hadn't spoken. "I regret that we couldn't wed. I hate the idea of that brute you married laying his hands on you. But that doesn't mean we can't still enjoy ourselves."

Her anger at the disparaging remark Robert made about her husband was quickly replaced by shock when she realized what he was saying. He didn't know her as well as she'd thought if he expected her to forgive him and agree to having an affair.

"I'm not here to talk about us. Not that there is anything between us anymore."

His smile could only be described as a smirk. "There could be. Don't pretend to be surprised. I always thought we were meant to be together. It's a pity your family's circumstances kept us apart, but you should know that my feelings for you remain unchanged."

Annoyance threatened to rob her of speech. "You made your feelings perfectly clear when you spurned me."

He made a soft tsking sound. "Still so bitter? I imagine your disappointment must have been great, especially when your parents forced you to wed that beast." His lips twisted in derision before he continued. "Oh yes, I know you very well, Sarah. How could I not? We've been friends for as long as I can remember. I could tell you wanted nothing more on your wedding day than to escape."

"Is that why you attended the breakfast? To make sure I was miserable without you?"

He shrugged. "You can hardly blame me for being curious about your new husband. But we both know you'll never care for him the same way you do for me."

Her stomach turned at Robert's overweening conceit. How had she never noticed his selfishness before now? And more importantly, how could she have imagined herself in love with him? She couldn't fathom that he expected her to believe he cared for her, not when it was evident that the only person he really cared about was himself.

She realized that he'd done her a great favor when he'd ended their courtship. She also recognized that this conversation was pointless. Robert Vaughan lived in his own world, one where he believed every member of the fairer sex would count themselves fortunate to receive even the smallest crumb of attention from him.

And, as always, he would do whatever he wanted. She'd just have to be vigilant about ensuring that Emily wasn't ensnared by him.

He moved so quickly she didn't realize his intentions until he'd pulled her into his arms. When his lips touched hers, anger galvanized her into action and she pushed him away.

"Don't say anything right now," he said, his hand against her mouth. She wanted to bite his fingers, but he pulled his hand away as soon as the thought entered her mind. "We'll speak again later."

Stunned into silence at his presumption, she could only stare after him as he sauntered from the room.

~

James finally managed to extricate himself from the card room where his father-in-law had demonstrated that he lacked any skill at all in playing cards. He also lacked the control to keep from playing and losing money everyone knew he didn't have. He'd have to do something about that, but later. Right now he was intent on finding Sarah and inviting her to dance with him.

He stood just inside the ballroom doors, his eyes scanning the guests, but couldn't find her. She wasn't with his mother and sister, nor was she dancing.

He headed back into the hallway, wondering if the Vaughans had opened another room for their guests' entertainment. He had just moved past a closed door when it swung open.

He turned in time to see Robert Vaughan exit the room, a satisfied air about him. Something about his expression and the fact that his wife was nowhere to be found set his senses on high alert. He couldn't stop replaying Mrs. Vaughan's voice over in his mind when she'd mentioned their past.

He took a step backward into the shadow of another doorway, waiting until Vaughan returned to the ball-room before making his way to the room the man had exited. With each step, he tried to convince himself that he was seeing betrayal where none existed.

The door was still open and he saw her before she noticed him. She was sitting in an armchair, looking down at her hands and breathing deeply. Trying to steady her breathing, he realized.

He stepped into the room and closed the door behind him. Sarah's gaze flew to his as she stood.

"What is the matter? You seem upset. Has something happened?"

Anger surged as he realized she was trying to play him for a fool. "I'd say discovering that my wife is having a secret assignation with a former lover qualifies me to be angry."

She stiffened at his words. "Robert and I were not lovers—you know that for a fact."

Hearing her use the other man's Christian name was like adding tinder to a flame. "Tell me, Sarah. Would that still be the case after tonight? Or perhaps you were merely making arrangements for a future encounter?"

Her chin tilted upward in defiance. "If you're worried about your heir, you needn't be. I know my duty, and I'll make sure I am with child before I look elsewhere."

Her cheeks were red, her fists clenched at her side. He couldn't tell if she was upset he'd caught her out or angry at his accusation. His heart ached to believe it was the latter, but she'd never given him any reason to think she cared for him outside the pleasure he could give her in the bedroom. It wasn't inconceivable that she'd seek out that same intimacy with the man she'd once loved. Perhaps still loved.

He turned and locked the door to ensure they wouldn't be interrupted. Sarah might still love Vaughan, but it was he who brought her to the heights of pleasure. She was his, and he wouldn't share her with anyone.

The sound of the lock clicking into place sounded unnaturally loud in the stillness that had descended after her declaration. He stalked toward his wife, satisfaction filling him when he saw the heat enter her eyes.

Well, at least she was no longer afraid of him.

CHAPTER 9

HAT WAS THE MATTER with her? Why on earth had she suggested that she would look outside her marriage for the intimacies she shared with him? Even if she still had feelings for Robert —and their recent conversation had shown her that those feelings were gone—she would never betray her wedding vows. She might not love James, but she respected him enough to remain faithful.

He'd been more shocked than anything when he'd accused her of arranging a romantic rendezvous with Robert, but now he was angry. The way his body had stiffened when she'd made her ridiculous statement, and the careful, measured steps he took as he stalked toward her, told her that her words had hit their mark. Despite the dim lighting in the room, she could see him clearly.

A part of her recognized that she should be afraid right now. Her stubborn pride had led her to provoke him with the one thing a man would never accept from his wife. But for some reason, she wasn't scared of her husband. Her head might tell her that she was playing with fire and was in grave danger of being burned, but her heart wanted him to deliver the sensual punishment she could see burning brightly in his eyes.

He stopped only inches from her. Her mind was telling her to proceed with caution, but her body was responding to his nearness. As he stared down at her, she found herself struggling to breathe, her nostrils filled with the scent that was uniquely his. Her heart was racing, but it wasn't from fear.

"I don't share, so you can put all thoughts of Vaughan or anyone else from your mind."

His breathing was almost as ragged as hers, the words spoken in a low, but deadly tone. And God help her, she almost swooned.

She couldn't say who moved first... She reached out to grasp his upper arms just as they came around her. His head descended, and when his lips met hers, she made a breathless sound of excitement. Gone was the tentative exploration he normally employed when he kissed her. The movement of his mouth against hers, the way his tongue thrust into her mouth, was dark, urgent. A corresponding desperation swelled within her as she raised her hands to wrap them around his neck and tried to draw him into her very skin. Seeking to tell him with her body what she could never tell him with words —that only he would ever touch her this way.

James turned with her in his arms and moved her backward. She assumed he was going to seat her on the small desk in the corner of the room, remembering how he had once made love to her on her dressing room table. She was surprised, therefore, when her back met a wall. No, not a wall. The door he'd locked.

He raised his head and stared down at her, his eyes almost black. "You're mine." His voice was low, dark. She should have been shocked when he started to lift her skirts, but instead she felt shivery and hot at the same time.

She urged his head back down to hers, and he came willingly. His hands didn't stop their movement, however. He hiked her skirts up to her hips and pressed his arousal against her mound. He was hard and huge, and her hands clutched at his shoulders. She tried to press herself more firmly against him but couldn't get close enough.

She knew he could bring her to fulfillment like this, by rubbing himself against her. It wasn't what she wanted, but she didn't imagine he'd take it further than that.

She was very wrong.

His hands left her hips briefly and she made a small sound of disappointment until she realized he'd shifted away from her to unbutton the fall of his trousers. Her heart was pounding, her body already eager to accept him. She wondered briefly if she was going mad. Surely it wasn't normal to be so desperate for another person that she didn't care that she was in a house filled with other people. The door was locked, and all that mattered to Sarah was getting closer to James. She wanted him inside her… needed him inside her. If he didn't ease the ache building within her, she would surely die.

She brought her mouth to the side of his neck and licked him there, just below his ear where his pulse beat an erratic rhythm. She was rewarded when he shuddered against her.

Her arms moved to wrap around his neck when he lifted her, and she made a soft sound of confusion when he kept her pressed against the door. She'd expected him to carry her to the desk.

His muscles bunched as he hooked one arm under her bottom and used the other to bring his hardness against her. He was poised at her entrance, the thick head brushing against her wetness, and she almost cried out in frustration when he raised his head to stare down at her.

"Who do you belong to, Sarah?"

He didn't have to ask her twice. She knew he sought her surrender, and she gave it willingly. Eagerly.

"You. Only to you."

He continued to stare down at her for several moments, some nameless emotion shifting behind his eyes. Captivating her. And then he pushed inside her, and she had to bury her head against his shoulder to keep from crying out at the delicious fullness.

He wasn't gentle, but gentleness was the last thing she needed. She needed the reminder that this was what their relationship was all about. She couldn't love her husband—she would never again allow another man to have that much power over her—but she could give him passion.

He thrust into her again and again, and some small part of her mind that wasn't swept away by James's lovemaking was grateful that the door was sturdy, making no sound as he drove into her.

Heat rose quickly, threatening to steal her breath as she raced toward release. When it came, she would have cried out if he hadn't taken her mouth in a kiss that lacked his normal finesse. He was continuing to thrust into her, his movements jerky, and as she rose to another peak, she was surprised that her desire had not been completely fulfilled.

She tore her mouth from his and leaned her forehead against his as he continued the onslaught. "What are you doing to me?" she murmured, her voice unsteady, their breath mingling.

He didn't reply, and her question was forgotten when she felt herself clenching against him again. This time she closed her eyes and pressed her teeth against her bottom lip to keep from crying out. Her breath hitched when he thrust into her one last time and released his seed deep within her.

They stayed like that for some time as their heartbeats slowed and their breathing returned to normal. When he pulled out of her and started putting his clothes back to rights, she almost moaned in disappointment. He handed her a handkerchief without a word. She took it, heat rising in her cheeks as she cleaned herself with quick, economical movements.

When she looked at him again, he was watching her, his arms folded across his massive chest. His expression was impossible to read. Their gazes held for several seconds before he spoke. "Will you be ready to return to the festivities soon?"

It took her a few seconds to realize what he'd just said, so great was her confusion. Surely he didn't expect her to return to the Christmas party after the heated encounter they'd just shared? A quick look down at herself told her that her dress was wrinkled, and she didn't even want to imagine the state of her hair. Everyone would know what had happened between them with just one look. James, however, looked as impeccable as ever.

"I don't think I can face everyone out there."

He scowled. "Everyone or Vaughan?"

This time she didn't allow her temper to goad her into saying something she didn't mean. "Everyone. I smell like you… They'll guess what we've been doing."

The corners of his mouth lifted in unmistakable satisfaction. "We're married, love. I think most people already know what goes on between a husband and a wife."

Normally his flippant attitude would have annoyed her, but his endearment unsettled her.

"Please, James."

He stared at her intently for several seconds before relenting. "I'll arrange to have the carriage brought around and then tell Mother and Emily that we're leaving. The carriage can return for them if they wish to stay a little longer."

She reached for his hand and squeezed it gently before releasing it again. The small gesture didn't change the way she'd jabbed at him, or the fact that they'd just been intimate in someone else's home—the Vaughans', no less—but she didn't miss the way his eyes softened.

"I fear I look a frightful mess. I need to visit the ladies' retiring room, after which I'll wait for you in the entryway."

He brushed the back of his fingers over her cheek, and an unsettling warmth spread through her as he said, "You could never be anything but beautiful."

CHAPTER 10

Christmas 1812

*A*s James reached up to loosen his cravat, he realized he was nervous. Which was absurd, really, but it felt like he had more at stake that morning. He knew he could take his wife to the heights of pleasure physically. He had yet to discover whether he could please her in other ways.

He glanced around the breakfast table, taking in his family. Sarah sat opposite him, his mother and sister on each side. Later that morning, Sarah's parents and her brother would join them. The only person missing was his brother Edward. James had received a letter the week before that the British army had retreated to Portugal for the winter. When he'd received the missive, he'd hoped that it contained news his brother was returning home. He should have known better. Edward was committed to doing his part to defeat Napoleon, and aside from becoming injured, only victory would lead him to retire his commission.

Emily nudged his arm, bringing him back to the present. "If you're insisting we wait until after breakfast to open presents, the least you can do is actually eat." She glared at his untouched plate.

Sarah laughed, a sound that never failed to touch him. It warmed his heart to see how well she got along with his family.

"I'm afraid I'm going to have to agree with Emily," she said, smiling at him before glancing at Emily with affection.

"Never say I wouldn't do everything possible to please the women in my family," he said, taking a large forkful of eggs.

Sarah's eyes met his, and he almost choked at the heat he saw reflected there. His thoughts immediately went to the previous night, and he knew she was remembering it as well. She had just finished her monthly courses, and after being away from her for several days, he'd been insatiable.

He wasn't even embarrassed when his mother cleared her throat, breaking their connection, and changed the subject.

Emily dragged them into the drawing room as soon as the meal was over. He almost suggested they wait until Sarah's family arrived, but before he could open his mouth to do so, Sarah touched his arm.

"Mama said they would exchange presents before leaving. They won't expect us to wait for them."

He nodded, robbed of speech for a moment. Sarah was so beautiful that morning—her hair a riot of curls, a festive yellow morning dress reflecting the gold in her hair. He wanted to draw her into his arms, but since they weren't alone he settled for bringing her hand to his lips.

An odd expression crossed her face, and it took him a moment to realize it was tenderness. Directed at him, not at something amusing his sister had said. His heart stuttered.

"Come on, you two," Emily said, dragging him away from his wife. "I've waited long enough. Now sit while I hand out the presents."

A footman had brought in the gifts while the family was at breakfast, and Emily headed straight for the pile of brightly wrapped boxes that was carefully arranged on a table placed next to the fireplace.

James took a moment to gaze around the room—the mantel groaning under the weight of festive greenery, his mother seated next to Sarah on the settee while Emily searched for a particular gift. His heart felt almost full to overflowing.

He was still nervous about his gift. He'd consulted Emily about it, wanting to ensure he gave Sarah something she'd enjoy. But now he wondered if it was enough. Perhaps he should have gotten her jewelry instead.

"I know you'll both appreciate the extreme sacrifice I'm making in waiting for the two of you to go first," Emily said, dropping colorfully wrapped packages in his and Sarah's laps. Her eyes glowed and she winked at him as she stepped back a few paces to wait. She was almost vibrating with excitement.

Sarah looked at him, but he waved his hand at the box in her lap. "I insist you go first."

It was the gentlemanly thing to do, but in reality he was beset by doubt. He'd placed so much importance on getting her something she would like, and now he worried that he'd failed. He needed to get her gift out of the way so he could enjoy the rest of the day.

As Sarah began to unwrap his present, his hands clenched involuntarily. He barely managed to keep from mangling the gift on his lap as he waited, suddenly certain that he hadn't done enough.

Unlike Emily, who usually tore the wrapping off her presents, Sarah carefully removed the paper, setting it aside before opening the wooden box. She stared at the contents for several long moments, and James's stomach dropped. She hated it.

When she looked up at him, her eyes were wide with wonder. "You got me oil paints."

"I know you love to draw and paint. Emily mentioned that you'd always wanted to try oil, but your parents insisted you limit yourself to watercolors. It seemed a shame that you not indulge your talent."

She stared at him, and he wondered if he'd misspoken.

Needing to fill the silence that had descended, he rushed on. "I've also arranged to have the room next to the gallery set up as your studio. It faces south and receives sunlight for a good portion of the day."

He stopped talking when she placed the box on the tea table and stood. He set aside his own gift and followed suit. "If you'd rather have jewels…"

She threw her arms around him and placed a kiss on his cheek. "They're perfect," she said after several seconds, leaning back to beam up at him.

"You're perfect," he replied, his voice low enough so only she could hear. Color rose in her cheeks, and her smile made his heart feel a thousand times lighter.

He released her reluctantly, and she turned to lift the flat box he'd set aside. "Now it's your turn."

He accepted the gift again and waited for her to sit before lowering himself into his chair.

"You have everything a man could possibly want," Sarah said as he tore the paper on his gift. "I thought, perhaps, you might enjoy this. It isn't much."

James didn't really care what she'd given him. It was enough that he'd made her happy.

His grin widened when he realized that she'd given him a picture. Not a watercolor, but one she'd drawn with colored pencils. It was a striking likeness of Rakehell, the prize stallion he'd brought with him when he'd taken up residence at Hathaway Park.

When he glanced back at Sarah, he could tell she was nervous. "I knew you were talented, but I grossly underestimated your ability. I'll definitely be framing this."

Sarah's smile wobbled, and he lifted a brow in question.

"There's a second picture below that one."

If it was even half as good as the first, his wife had no reason to be concerned. Curious, he lifted the top page. When his gaze fell on the second picture, he froze. There, on the paper, was a drawing of him. He was at the stables, a hand on Rakehell's mane as he leaned close to speak to the animal.

His mind went back to the day it was drawn. Sarah and Emily had visited the stables, and he'd been very aware of her presence as he'd gone about his work. Emily had been chattering nonstop while Sarah drew, but he'd had no idea she was drawing him.

"So this is why you and Emily were out at the stables that day."

"I couldn't think of what to give one of the wealthiest men in all of England. Since I know how much you love your horses…" She shrugged.

It wasn't the horse in the picture that had captured his attention but the way she'd drawn him. There was a light in his eyes and a grin on his face that almost made him appear handsome. Was that how Sarah saw him? Or had she made him appear more handsome than he really was? As his eyes scanned the drawing, however, he saw that she'd accurately captured the slight bend in his nose from the time he'd broken it trying to tame a particularly stubborn stallion. And it didn't appear as though she'd altered any of his features for the better.

Yet, somehow, she'd made him appear more handsome than he knew he was.

"I don't know what to say."

"Do you like it?" She was biting her lip, and he wanted nothing more at that moment than to draw her onto his lap and show her just how much he liked it. How much she'd taken away his breath with her thoughtfulness.

Their eyes met and held. "I will treasure this."

What he didn't tell Sarah was that looking at the drawing gave him hope that she would one day come to care for him. Perhaps even love him.

"Now it's our turn," Emily said, capturing his attention. He'd almost forgotten he and Sarah weren't alone. "Mama and I also got you presents, but if I don't open that large box over there with my name on it, I'm going to expire from curiosity."

James laughed, his heart feeling a hundred times lighter than when he'd entered the room. "By all means. I'd hate to be the cause of your distress."

Emily needed no more encouragement. She quickly handed out the rest of the gifts and then proceeded to tear open her present.

Before long, all the gifts were open and Emily was suggesting they head into the music room to sing Christmas carols.

They would be leaving for Christmas service later that morning, after Sarah's family arrived. James wanted to spirit Sarah away and thank her properly, but that would have to wait until later that evening when everyone had gone. James steeled himself for the long day ahead. Much as he loved his family, he looked forward to exploring whether Sarah's gift contained the hidden meaning he wanted to ascribe to it.

HAPPINESS SETTLED over Sarah as they proceeded to the music room. She hadn't wanted to admit to herself that she'd been worried about her husband's reaction to her small gift. What did one give someone, after all, who already had everything? He loved nothing better than his stables, and Emily had assured her that her brother would enjoy the drawings.

The way he'd looked at her after opening her gift had flustered her. It was the same look he gave her when he joined her in the bedroom. And while Emily and Mrs. Hathaway were opening their own presents, she'd glanced his way more than a few times to find him staring at her. She couldn't help but wonder what he was thinking.

Emily urged her to play the first song, and Sarah had to take a few deep breaths as she settled before the pianoforte. It wouldn't do to mangle the song she was about to play because she was distracted by thoughts of her husband.

"I hope you'll all join me," she said as she shifted over on the bench so Emily could sit next to her. "I can manage playing, but my voice is only passable at best."

"Oh, never fear," Emily said, giving her a small hug

as she sat next to her. "Singing carols on Christmas morning is a family tradition. We'll all join in."

"Even James?" It had never occurred to her to wonder if her husband could sing. Her own brother and father loathed the activity, which was understandable given that neither could carry a tune.

"Oh yes," Mrs. Hathaway said, beaming with pride at her son. "He has a very nice singing voice. I admit that he puts Emily and me to shame."

"I shall be the judge of that," Sarah said with mock seriousness as she began to play "God Rest Ye Merry, Gentlemen," one of the few carols she knew well enough to play by memory.

She'd thought her mother-in-law was exaggerating her son's talents, but when James's smooth baritone joined in, she found herself gaping at him in shock, almost losing her place in the song. He winked at her, knowing full well that he had surprised her.

"Mama never lies," Emily said when they'd reached the end of the carol.

"I can see that," Sarah said, shifting over on the bench so Emily could play the next song.

They were interrupted by the soft murmur of voices coming from the hallway, indicating that Sarah's family had arrived. She rose and had just reached James's side when the footman announced them.

Sarah greeted her mother and brother with heartfelt hugs but hesitated when she saw the stern set of her father's jaw. She dropped into a brief curtsy in front of him, hating the relief that flooded through her when she didn't detect a hint of spirits. It embarrassed her that it wasn't outside the realm of possibility for her father to have already started drinking this early in the morning.

She watched James greet her parents and brother, the happiness of the day disappearing when she noticed the way her father glared at James.

Her eyes flew to George's, and her brother gave a short, abbreviated shake of his head, their signal to each other that their father was in a mood and would be quick to anger.

As usual, her mother attempted to make up for her father's rudeness by greeting everyone warmly and throwing herself into the activity they'd interrupted. Sarah didn't resume her seat at the pianoforte, choosing to sit next to her mother while Emily played.

She tried to concentrate on the next carol. She didn't expect her father and brother to join in, but James's rich voice seemed to wrap around her, giving her a measure of comfort. That comfort was quickly ripped away when he stopped singing midway through the song.

She turned in time to see her father say something to him, then the two men stood and left the room. She looked at George, wondering if he knew what was happening, but he only shrugged in reply. Her mother gave no indication that she had noticed the men's departure, but Sarah knew that her calm demeanor was only a mask. Her mother was always one to avoid conflict, and she wouldn't want to draw attention to whatever it was that had upset her father.

For several moments, Sarah wrestled with what to do. When she stood, her mother reached out to grasp her hand, giving a small shake of her head. That small motion, however, convinced Sarah that she needed to learn what was happening. She wouldn't have admitted it, but she was suddenly worried for James.

She heard her father's raised voice the moment she stepped into the hallway and made sure to close the door to the music room behind her. She found the two men in the drawing room.

James was standing just inside the doorway, facing her father who was pacing as he ranted about something. When he noticed her, his shoulders stiffened.

"You should return to the music room," James said.

Her father spun around at his comment and pinned Sarah with an angry glare. "Do you know what your husband has done?"

"With all due respect, Sir Henry, I don't think Sarah needs to be present for this discussion."

Her father snorted with disgust. "So you've deceived her as you have me?"

"There was no deception," James replied, his voice calm despite the other man's anger. Sarah had detected the slight hesitation before he spoke, and she couldn't help but wonder what it was that James didn't want her to know.

"He's made it known that no one is to accept credit from me. Do you know what that means?"

Sarah knew exactly what it meant and silently applauded her husband's foresight.

"It means you can no longer drive your family into debt. I would prefer, of course, if you could manage your own money, but since it's clear that you cannot, I've had to take steps to ensure there's still an estate left to bequeath to your son."

Her father's face turned an alarming shade of red, and for a moment, she feared that James had pushed her father too far.

"It is Christmas Day, Papa. Surely this conversation can wait until another time."

Silence descended upon the room, and Sarah held her breath as she waited for her father's reply.

"You'll speak to your husband on my behalf, right, Sarah?" her father said, turning to face her.

"Of course," she said, relieved that her father was being reasonable. It didn't happen often, but he wasn't in his cups, which normally helped his mood.

He nodded stiffly, moving past her to leave the room. Sarah waited until she heard the music room door being opened, the festive music spilling out into the hallway momentarily before her father closed it again.

When she turned back to face James, she was surprised to see he was still tense. Confused, she placed a hand on his arm to set him at ease. "Thank you."

His brows drew together in a slight frown. "You're not upset with me?"

His demeanor made sense now. He'd expected her to censure him for his behavior.

"We both know my father has no self-control. I'll admit I've been worried for George. Once you'd paid all of Papa's debts, I expected him to run up new ones." She gave her head a slight shake. "He'll always hold a grudge against you for this though. And I'm sure he'll seek out ways to continue his gambling."

"I might be able to help with that. It seems that having a title—and the obscene wealth that comes with this one, in particular—actually gives me some influence with others. I've already let it be known that anyone who allows him to run up any future debts won't receive so much as a shilling from me. For some reason people care about my displeasure. I'll admit, it's an odd sensation."

Sarah smiled as she saw him wrestle with the notion before shaking it off. She almost told him that she cared about his feelings but held herself back at the last moment.

"We've only postponed your father's ire. He won't thank me when he learns I didn't allow my wife to cajole me from my decision."

"You don't have to shield me," Sarah said, oddly touched that her husband would take all the blame upon himself.

"Nonsense. Your father is already angry with me. I doubt he could be more so. There's no reason for him to turn that anger onto you." He held out his arm and Sarah took it automatically. "What say you, should we try to enjoy the rest of this day?"

Warmth spread through Sarah, replacing the dread she'd felt when she entered the room. "I'd say that is an excellent suggestion."

CHAPTER 11

May 1813

SARAH SPENT THE NEXT few months waiting for her father to upset the peace that had settled over their household since Christmas. He was too set in his ways to change, and over the years she'd learned from her mother—who treated her more like a confidante than a child who needed to be sheltered from the realities of life—that he had a talent for finding people to lend him money. Money he would then proceed to lose at an alarming rate. James had put a halt to that temporarily, but she worried that her father would find a way to return to his old habits.

Instead, the disturbance came from an entirely unexpected quarter... her former suitor.

It was early afternoon when Sarah was told she had a caller. As he was most days now that the construction of the new stables was reaching an end, James was away from home.

Expecting her mother, Sarah made her way to the drawing room. When she entered the room, however, she was dismayed to find Robert waiting for her.

His audacity left her stunned for a moment as she remembered the last time she'd seen him and the impertinent suggestion he'd made. How had she forgotten that moment or the fact that he'd tried to kiss her? But then, given the vigorous and often inventive ways her husband had used to distract her since that evening, it wasn't surprising that Robert would be the last person on her mind.

Robert rose when she entered the room and she couldn't help but notice that he had taken great care with his appearance. But then Sarah had never seen him with so much as a hair out of place. She couldn't help but contrast his fastidiousness to her husband's more casual attitude toward fashion and was surprised to find that the man who stood before her now—his fair hair neatly swept back, his royal-blue coat carefully matched to the color of his eyes—no longer impressed her.

In the few short months of their marriage, she'd come to appreciate the confident ease with which her husband carried himself. James liked to loosen his cravat as the day progressed and never bothered to wear a tailcoat when they weren't expecting callers. He did start the day with a waistcoat, but even that concession to formality was often discarded at some point during the day.

Clearing her mind from the wayward thoughts that sprang to mind with the realization of just how much she enjoyed watching her husband loosen up as the day progressed, she forced a smile and inclined her head.

"Good afternoon," she said, pleased that she'd managed to keep her voice even.

A slight frown creased Robert's brow at her cool manner, but he bowed briefly and waited for her to take a seat on the settee. Instead of resuming his seat, he crossed the space between them and lowered himself onto the settee next to her. She had to stifle the impulse to stand and move to one of the chairs, knowing that Robert would take her action as proof she was still affected by his nearness when the opposite was true.

"I am surprised you are here."

He smiled at her, and a spark of alarm ignited within her when she saw the mischief in his eyes. "Aren't you going to offer me refreshments, Sarah? I think the company you've been keeping of late hasn't improved your manners."

Somehow she held back the rebuke that sprang to her lips. It wouldn't do to make an enemy of this man, not when she was already worried about the motivation for his visit. It was entirely possible, after all, that Robert was here because he was hoping to get closer to Emily.

But the last thing she would do was give him reason to stay longer than necessary and risk having James return to find them alone together. Again.

"I trust your parents are well?"

Robert pursed his lips in a moue of disappointment,

and Sarah felt a stab of irritation at the affectation. "Come now, let us not pretend to be mere acquaintances exchanging polite pleasantries. I think you know why I am here."

She'd almost convinced herself that he was there to see Emily, but the way his eyes kept creeping down to her décolletage suggested otherwise. Much as she hated his presumption, she was relieved that she'd been mistaken. She could handle Robert. Emily, however, was far too young and innocent, and she feared it would take very little effort on Robert's part to cause her sister-in-law to fall in love with him.

"Don't be coy, Robert. You know I don't enjoy guessing games."

He made a soft tsking sound and gave her a meaningful look. "I'm here about my proposal."

She wasn't surprised. Robert always did think that the world revolved around him. Still, his audacity almost took away her breath. "You would actually approach me here, in my husband's home, to suggest I betray my wedding vows?"

Robert lifted a shoulder in a casual shrug. "Your husband's habits are very predictable. He's so enamored with the construction of his new stables—" The twist of his lips told her clearly what he thought of her husband's plans to continue breeding horses. "He won't even know I was here. But if you prefer, we can make arrangements to meet elsewhere. I know you'll be leaving for Town soon. It shouldn't be too difficult to arrange a meeting while you're there."

He ended with a broad wink, and Sarah was almost embarrassed for him. How could he be so delusional as to think she would fall into his arms after the way he had cast her aside? Clearly he thought himself so irresistible that she would be content to accept whatever scraps of attention he chose to give her.

"You would be mistaken." Her husband's voice came from the doorway, and with a gasp she turned to see him standing there, the breadth of his shoulders almost encompassing the whole opening. Sarah had never seen James's eyes so cold and hard. From the way he was clenching his fists, it was clear he'd heard enough of their conversation to know the reason for Robert's visit.

Robert leaped to his feet. "I'm not sure what you think you heard—"

"I heard you propositioning my wife." James moved into the room, his anger palpable in the tense atmosphere that settled over the room. Wisely, Robert took a step back, but he wasn't quick enough to escape her husband. James grabbed him roughly by the throat and bent Robert's right arm behind his back. The slighter man clutched at James's arm with his left hand, but he was powerless to move him.

Shocked at James's display of anger, Sarah stood on shaky legs and could only watch, frozen, as he yanked Robert closer to him.

"If you wish to live to see another day, you will put all thoughts of my wife behind you. If your paths should cross in public, you will acknowledge her as is befitting her station and then continue on your way." His face was now mere inches away from Robert's. "But if I ever find you alone with her again—or learn that you've been alone with her, and you can rest assured that I *will* hear about it—I will take great pleasure in making sure you regret that action. Do I make myself clear?"

A gurgle of sound emerged from Robert's throat, but he nodded his assent with a frantic, jerky movement, his eyes wild with terror.

For one heart-stopping moment, Sarah wasn't sure James would release Robert. When he finally did, he flung him away and Robert stumbled backward. Sarah cried out, visions of Robert lying in a broken heap on the floor crowding her mind.

James cast her a look that threatened to steal her breath, for in it she saw hurt. He believed she would betray him. And why wouldn't he? She'd never told him what had actually taken place between her and Robert at the Vaughans' Christmas party. Instead, she'd allowed her husband to continue to believe the words that her foolish pride had spurred her to utter... that she would one day betray him.

He turned and glared at Robert as he scurried from the room. They remained frozen in place—James facing the doorway and Sarah staring at his back—as they listened to the sound of the front door opening and slamming closed.

When James turned to face her again, the hurt she'd glimpsed was gone. In its place there remained only anger.

"I need to explain—"

"Don't." The harshly spoken word stopped her in her tracks.

"But that wasn't what it seemed—"

His harsh laugh caused an odd shifting sensation somewhere in the vicinity of her heart.

"I don't need your explanations. Your actions have spoken volumes."

With that, he turned and strode from the room.

As she watched him retreat from her, clarity entered her mind. She realized that she'd done the very thing she'd vowed never to allow—she'd fallen in love with her husband. Even worse, she'd led him to believe that she was the type of woman to whom he could never entrust his own heart.

Her legs gave way and she collapsed onto the settee. How could she have allowed that to happen? And more importantly, how was she going to protect herself from this new heartbreak?

HAVING GROWN up with a father who railed against any slight, whether real or imagined, Sarah thought she'd prefer the polite distance James now showed her. It came as a shock, therefore, to discover that his icy demeanor had an agonizing effect on her emotions.

She couldn't stop thinking about the hurt she'd seen in his eyes and hated herself for having caused it. She tried on several occasions to explain that she had no intention of betraying her marriage vows. After he cut her off for the third time, she realized the effort was futile and stopped trying to raise the subject. There was another subject she wanted to raise with James, but the distance between them made it impossible.

That week dragged by slowly, made even longer by the fact that James didn't visit her at night. She tried to occupy her time with preparations for their trip to London, but there wasn't a great deal for her to do. They'd only be staying a few days before heading to the Earl of Sanderson's estate just outside of Town to attend his wedding to James's aunt.

She attempted to escape into the little artist's studio James had set up for her but found that drawing or painting brought her no joy. Her heart ached each time she looked at the set of oil paints her husband had given her at Christmas. She could only hope that getting away from this house, away from reminders of what her husband thought he had witnessed, would ease the strain between them.

She counted on Emily and her mother-in-law's presence to help defuse the tension during the trip to London. When the date for the departure arrived, however, she was disappointed to learn that only she and James would be making the journey. Mrs. Hathaway had fallen ill with the grippe and Emily was to stay behind to care for her mother.

The trip to town was made in one day with a short, awkward break at an inn for a midday meal. If Sarah had thought the week leading up to that day was long, it was nothing to riding alone within the stifling interior of the Hathaway coach. Instead of keeping her company, James chose to spend the majority of the trip on horseback.

Sarah had hoped the enforced confinement of their trip would allow her to share the news she had received the day before. The doctor had visited while James was at the stables and confirmed her suspicion that she was with child. She wanted to tell James, but it was impossible when he went out of his way to avoid her company.

By the time the carriage arrived at James's town house—a residence that was much larger than the other houses in the very fashionable Mayfair neighborhood—dusk was falling and exhaustion pulled at her. She hadn't been able to sleep during the journey, her mind spinning as she tried to imagine how James would react upon hearing her news. A part of her wondered if he'd already learned of the doctor's visit. Did he already suspect she was with child and just not care?

She tried to push that horrible thought away, but it was impossible to keep from dwelling on the negative. Especially when James didn't take her arm after helping her down from the carriage.

The butler opened the front door just as they reached it. This was Sarah's first visit to the Hathaway town house, and she braced herself for the inevitable introduction to the staff. Fortunately, the servants weren't as numerous as at Hathaway Park and that formality was soon over.

Finally Sarah allowed her curiosity free rein and wandered into the drawing room. She could only stare, amazed that the decor was even more ostentatious than that of the estate. The marble floor was polished to a mirrorlike shine, and the walls were covered in a paper that, if she wasn't mistaken, actually had gold embossing. She tried to imagine what the rest of the house would look like and found that her imagination wasn't up to the task.

"I didn't think it was possible for any house to be more ornate than Hathaway Park."

"I thought you'd like it," James said, his eyes cold as he stared at her. "But you did agree to marry me for my money, after all."

It was the most he'd said to her in days, and she barely caught herself from flinching as the harsh words tore through her.

She didn't reply, needing desperately to get away from James before she broke down into tears. She turned to the butler, who was standing off to the side, pretending not to have heard James's insult.

"I'd like to see my room now. I find that I'm quite fatigued from the journey." She turned back to James, adding, "If you'll excuse me, I'll have a tray sent up to my room."

James frowned, but in that moment Sarah didn't care if he could see just how much his words had wounded her. As she followed the butler up the stairs to her bedroom, she could feel the weight of her husband's gaze on her back. She made sure to keep her spine straight and her head held high.

CHAPTER 12

TWO AGONIZING DAYS had dragged by since their arrival in London. Interminable days during which Sarah only saw her husband at dinner. She filled the time by becoming acquainted with the staff and the manner in which the town house was run. They wouldn't be staying long enough for her to impose any changes, but it soon became apparent that none were needed. She wasn't surprised since she knew how fastidious James's uncle had been. With her marriage, she might just have inherited one of the best staffs in all of London, rivaled only by the small army employed in the upkeep of Hathaway Park.

She tried to pass the time sketching but was acutely aware of every minute that passed without seeing her husband. At night she waited for him to join her but dropped, alone, into an exhausted sleep. Faced with James's cool demeanor at dinner, she still hadn't been able to bring herself to tell him that she was increasing.

When the morning of the wedding of the dowager Viscountess Hathaway finally arrived, Sarah found herself alone in the carriage with her husband. Unlike their journey to Town, James chose not to ride alongside the carriage. She knew him well enough now to realize he was self-conscious about how others perceived him. He wouldn't want to arrive at the wedding smelling like the stables.

She spent that hour-long drive buffeted by emotion. Wanting to reach out to her husband, tell him that she did not see him as wanting... that, in fact, she found him more noble than most of the men of her acquaintance. Yet fear that he'd scorn her outpouring of sentiment held her back.

Or worse, that he'd laugh at her for hoping that his feelings for her went beyond enjoying their time in bed together. She couldn't shake the suspicion that he didn't actually like her since she hadn't seen any indication that he wanted to know her outside of the bedroom.

Well, except for his behavior on Christmas morning. She hadn't even realized that he'd given any thought to her love for drawing and painting. Surely a man who'd gone to the effort to give her something so meaningful must care for her, even if just a little.

Their arrival at the Earl of Sanderson's estate brought an end to her internal turmoil. As the carriage drew to a halt, she glanced sideways at James, where he sat looking out the carriage window, and sighed. Even if she couldn't tell him about her emotions, she'd have to find the courage to breach the distance between them and tell him he would soon be a father.

James held himself stiffly, an indication that the trip had been equally uncomfortable for him. Despite that, Sarah couldn't help but admire how handsome he was as she drank in his profile. Her fingers itched to explore the hard muscles that lay beneath the fabric of his waistcoat. She wanted to trail her hand upward, ease the stiffness of his jaw, see his mouth curve into that wicked smile he gave her when he was about to make love to her.

She ached from the need coursing through her in that moment.

Her heart fell when the carriage drew to a halt and James remained seated, waiting for a footman to open the carriage door and help her down instead of preceding her and handling that task himself. She hadn't realized until that moment how much she'd been looking forward to that small amount of physical contact from him.

As it was almost time for the marriage ceremony, they were greeted by one of the earl's sisters. After welcoming them, she summoned a footman to show them to their bedroom. She and James would be staying the night before returning to Hathaway Park in Northampton on the morrow.

James barely entered the room they were to share, remaining just inside the doorway when the footman left to collect the one trunk they'd packed for their brief stay and to summon a maid to help Sarah dress.

127

James cleared his throat before meeting her gaze. "The ceremony will begin in just over an hour. I'll leave you now to…" James faltered only momentarily, but it was enough to tell Sarah that her husband could hardly wait to quit her company. "I'll return to fetch you when it's time."

"You needn't put yourself out," she said, unable to hold back her own annoyance. Really, was it so difficult for him to pretend that he could tolerate her presence? "I'm sure a footman will be able to show me the way to the chapel."

He offered her a curt nod before turning and leaving her alone. The sound of the door closing behind him sounded unnaturally loud in the still room. Sarah let out a silent scream of annoyance and flung herself onto the bed. Her waspishness toward her husband certainly wasn't helping the situation, but if he'd wanted a meek wife who would be content to have whatever scrap of attention he threw her way with nary a word or raised brow, he'd married the wrong woman.

An hour later, Sarah found herself following another footman to the chapel situated a short walk north of the Sanderson estate. She'd managed to steady her nerves, and she was determined to close the gap that had grown between her and James.

The maid who had been sent up to help her dress had teased her hair out from the practical knot she'd worn for the carriage ride. Thankfully, her natural curls didn't require a lot of attention, and now they framed her face in what she knew was a becoming manner. She'd chosen to wear a deep blue gown that was cut just low enough to showcase her breasts and she knew the color complemented her fair coloring. She didn't bother trying to deny to herself that she was hoping to ensnare James's attention. They were sharing a room for the night, after all. Surely when they retired for the evening, he'd finally make love to her again. Afterward, she'd tell him about her condition.

James was waiting outside the chapel and when he saw her, his eyes dropped to her bodice. Instead of the desire she'd hoped to see when he lifted his gaze to hers again, his expression was carefully neutral. She squelched her disappointment and smiled at him when she took his arm, her heartbeat sounding unnaturally loud to her own ears as they entered the chapel.

IT WAS MADDENING how much he wanted the woman standing by his side, the warmth of her small hand on his arm seeming to burn a hole through his coat. James had to struggle against the almost overwhelming need to draw Sarah into his arms.

The ride down from London had been bad enough, the intimate interior of the carriage ensuring he was aware of her every breath, the scent of her filling his nostrils. It had taken every ounce of willpower he possessed to leave the bedroom the footman had shown them to. Only the memory of the horrified expression on his wife's face when he'd threatened the man she still loved had given him the strength to turn away from her.

But it was clear to him now that this woman would always be his weakness. How he could still desire her even though he knew she wanted nothing to do with him was a mystery—one he feared he would never solve.

James's uncle had married a woman quite a few years younger than himself, hoping she'd give him a son to inherit the Hathaway title. Their marriage had lasted twelve years, but the union had not resulted in any offspring. Now, just thirteen months after his passing, Miranda Hathaway was marrying a man she appeared to love. It was equally clear to him that Sanderson was just as enamored of his wife-to-be. James was happy for the pair, but he couldn't help feeling a pang of envy.

The actual wedding ceremony wasn't long. Seeing the way Miranda and Sanderson looked at each other, James couldn't help but contrast the event to his own wedding to Sarah. She had done an admirable job of hiding her discomfort, but he'd been aware of it none-theless. He wondered how many other people had been aware of her reluctance to marry him.

Probably everyone.

Normally he tried not to think back to that day, but given his wife's recent behavior, it was impossible to ignore the fact that nothing had changed in the past six months of their marriage. Yes, she was a willing partner in the bedroom, but she hadn't given him any indication that her feelings for him had changed outside of that room. The hope he'd harbored after receiving her

Christmas gift had only proven how much of a fool he was when it came to his wife.

He had to endure the walk back to the estate for the wedding breakfast with Sarah clinging to his arm. In contrast to the way she had ignored him during their carriage ride that morning or the way she had snapped at him after they'd arrived, she seemed to be going out of her way to be pleasant to him. Much as he wanted to take her new behavior at face value, he knew she was only putting on a show for the other guests. He supposed he should be grateful. Marriages of convenience were common among the *ton* but he was very aware that he didn't fit in. Anyone witnessing her cool behavior toward him would assume—correctly—that she was miserable in her marriage and laid the blame squarely at his feet.

When she smiled at him before taking her seat at the breakfast table, he had to hold back the urge to tell her that she needn't pretend quite so prettily for his sake. Instead, he told himself that at least here he wouldn't have to worry about finding his wife alone, yet again, with the man she loved.

CHAPTER 13

*B*Y THE TIME Sarah retired for the night, her jaw ached from forcing herself to smile, and her head was pounding. The doctor had told her she would tire more easily because of her pregnancy, but she recognized that her fatigue stemmed from more than her physical condition.

As the maid helped her unbutton her dress and unlace her too-tight corset, she had to acknowledge that she was dejected by how the day had progressed. James had barely spoken to her during the wedding breakfast, and when it was over he'd taken his leave with a small bow. When the newly married couple had disappeared as well, she'd hoped to retire to their room and rest for a bit. But the earl's sisters had thwarted that plan, having scheduled several activities to occupy their guests.

She hadn't seen James again until dinner, which proved to be a dreadfully long affair. Worse, she'd had to sit opposite him and watch as another woman—a young widow to whom Sarah had taken an instant dislike—all but offered herself up to him.

She was seated next to a middle-aged, talkative gentleman, so she couldn't overhear her husband's conversation, but whatever they were discussing seemed to amuse James. Really, the way the woman leaned into him, even having the nerve to place her hand on James's arm while she laughed at everything he said, made Sarah want to climb over the dining room table and claw out her eyes.

She wanted to believe that her husband was putting on a show for her benefit, paying her back in kind for what he believed to be her transgressions with Robert. But the fact that he never glanced in her direction caused her to doubt that was his motivation. Surely if he were trying to make her jealous, he would have glanced at her at least once to gauge her reaction to his performance.

No, her stomach had turned into a dark knot of despair at the realization that he simply didn't care how she was taking their intimate tête-à-tête. In fact, he seemed not to be aware of her presence at all.

As she dismissed the maid and crawled into bed, she couldn't help but worry that it might already be too late to repair their relationship, let alone win James's affection. Too much time had passed and she'd given him no indication about her true feelings. It was entirely possible that he had given up on her.

She sighed. Had he even wanted her affection? She had no reason to believe he'd ever wanted anything from her other than a legitimate heir. What she'd taken as his jealousy toward Robert was, in all likelihood the behavior of someone trying to hold on to their pride. What man wanted to be cuckolded or to raise another man's child as his own? Certainly not James. He'd made that very clear on the day they'd wed.

She tried to remain awake, hoping that her husband would join her soon, but fatigue pulled her into a deep sleep almost at once. When she started awake the next morning, disappointment flooded through her.

She wasn't sure what she expected to find when she rose from the bed. Surely there would be some sign that her husband had spent the night in their shared bedroom even if he hadn't woken her. Rumpled sheets on the other side of the bed, a discarded cravat... something. Instead, she found the room as pristine as it had been when she'd retired. Had her husband returned to their room at all last night?

A suspicion, almost too horrible to contemplate, formed in her mind as she remembered the way James's dinner companion had blatantly flirted with him throughout the meal. Had James chosen, instead, to visit the widow's bedroom last night?

Pain lanced through her at the thought, so swift that it left her momentarily gasping for breath. Worse was the realization that when she told James she was carrying his child, he would no longer need to visit her bed. She'd hoped that would be the case when they'd first wed, but it hadn't taken long for her to become addicted to her husband's touch. More than that, she craved his attention. His love. But if the previous evening had shown her anything, it was that there were plenty of women willing to take her place.

She almost didn't hear the soft knock at the door so mired was she in fear that she had already been replaced. She had just enough time to turn away before the maid who had helped her the previous day entered the room. She quickly dashed the tears threatening to fall, took a deep breath, and turned to face the woman.

"I'm sorry to disturb you so early, my lady, but His Lordship left word that you would be departing early. A breakfast tray will be sent up shortly."

Sarah took small comfort from the thought that she'd be spared the sight of watching her husband pay court to another woman while she attempted to break her fast. Such a sight would have turned her stomach, not to mention what it would have done to her heart.

She tried to shake off her unease as the maid helped her dress. She'd have to face her husband soon, and she had no idea what she would say to him.

Another knock at the door just as the maid was leaving signaled the arrival of her meal. But instead of a footman, the tray was brought in by James's aunt.

"I hope you don't mind that I intercepted your breakfast. We haven't had the chance to get to know one another, and since you and James will be leaving shortly, I knew this would be my only opportunity to remedy that oversight."

"Not at all," Sarah said, taking the tray and carrying it to her dressing table. "I welcome the opportunity."

Miranda moved to the chaise and sat. James's aunt was only a few years older than him and still a very beautiful woman. Her dark hair was pulled up into a simple but elegant knot, her gray eyes almost too large for her face. Sarah could almost feel those eyes looking deep into her soul.

"There's only one cup," Sarah said. "I can ring for another one—"

Miranda shook her head. "I've already eaten this morning."

When Sarah hesitated, uncertain whether the other woman intended to watch her eat, Miranda let out a sigh.

"I'm sorry, it appears I've made you nervous. That wasn't my intention." She shifted on the chaise. "Come sit next to me. I'll only be a moment, then I'll leave you to finish your meal."

Sarah did as the other woman requested, feeling as though she was about to be brought to task for some transgression.

"Oh dear, I'm only making things worse. Excuse me for being blunt, but I have to ask. Do you care for my nephew?"

Sarah considered lying, her first instinct to protect her pride. But she was tired of pushing people away. If she hadn't been so determined to keep her husband at arm's length, she might not be in the sorry situation in which she now found herself.

"I didn't expect to, but much to my surprise, I do."

"Andrew told me not to get involved, but I couldn't

help but notice that things are tense between you and James."

Sarah wanted nothing more than for the floor to open up and swallow her whole. What could she say that wasn't already evident to everyone who saw the two of them together?

"Does James know how you feel?"

Sarah hadn't expected this line of questioning. If she'd been asked, she would have said that she'd do everything in her power to ensure it never took place. But in that moment, she needed to speak to someone. She couldn't confide in his family, and she didn't want to burden her mother with the knowledge that she was so unhappy.

Sarah shook her head. "He believes that I care for someone else." She rushed to explain when she saw the frown on the other woman's face. "There was an unspoken understanding between myself and another, but that ended before my marriage. I'll admit, I entered the marriage not expecting to care for James, but somewhere along the way my feelings changed."

Miranda covered her hands, which she hadn't realized she was clutching together in her lap.

"Would you like me to speak to him on your behalf?"

Sarah hated the pity she saw on the other woman's face. "And say what? It is clear to everyone that you and Lord Sanderson care deeply for one another, but most marriages aren't love matches."

Miranda seemed to weigh her words before speaking. "Andrew believes that my nephew cares for you."

Sarah couldn't hold back her mirthless laugh at that bit of absurdity despite the fact that the other woman's words had caused her heart to clench. "Oh, he likes me well enough in bed. It's all the other times when he can't bear to even look at me."

Miranda would understand how such marriages worked. She, herself, had been in a similar marriage to the former Viscount Hathaway before his death had left her a widow.

Miranda squeezed Sarah's hand again before releasing it. "I really don't think that's true. Perhaps it's time for you to take a chance and tell him how you feel." Sarah was about to protest, but Miranda continued. "Would you really be more unhappy if you tried and failed than you are right now?"

Sarah honestly couldn't answer that question.

Miranda gave her a quick hug, then stood and took her leave.

Sarah sat there for several minutes, unable to banish Miranda's words from her mind. She wasn't sure if she could summon up the courage to tell James that she loved him, but it was time for him to learn that he might soon be getting his heir.

JAMES REGRETTED his decision to ride in the carriage

with his wife almost as soon as they left Sanderson's estate. It wasn't so much Miranda's comment about how tedious the journey home would be for Sarah alone in the carriage that had him changing his mind but the look of disappointment on Miranda's face when he'd started to tell her that he would be riding alongside the carriage. He knew that his aunt and her new husband were in love, and it was clear that Miranda hoped the same was true of his marriage. For some reason he couldn't fathom, she seemed oddly insistent that James remain with his wife.

The carriage felt even more cramped than it had on their trip to Sanderson's estate the previous morning. He was acutely aware of his wife's presence, and he decided that he'd been away from her for too long. It was almost two weeks since they'd made love, something which he planned to correct that evening after their return.

Until then, thoughts of what he wanted to do with her plagued him.

Last night had been hell. He'd retired very late in order to avoid Sarah. She'd been going to bed earlier of late, and by the time he'd returned to their shared bedroom, she'd been asleep. He'd spent a miserable night on the chaise longue, battling the urge to crawl into bed with her. He'd finally given up trying to get any real rest at about five in the morning and had dressed quickly—thankful that he'd never had a valet until recently—and ventured downstairs.

He'd been successful in his aim to show Sarah that while she might not love him, he could bring her physical satisfaction. Now he couldn't help but worry that she would seek that satisfaction with another man. Vaughan. The thought of the other man's smug face had him clenching his hands.

The intimacy within the carriage was too much to bear and his nerves were on edge. Better that he spend the rest of the trip sitting next to the carriage driver outside. He raised a hand to rap on the roof of the carriage but stopped just short when his wife cleared her throat.

"Are you leaving?"

"I thought I'd get some air. I didn't get much sleep last night, and the morning air should keep me from falling asleep."

She looked away at his words, and for a brief moment he thought he could detect a hint of hurt on her face. It disappeared almost instantly, and he chided himself for thinking he could have any sway over her emotions.

"I have something important to tell you." Sarah met his gaze and this time, by the way she clenched her hands together in her lap, he could tell she was worried.

He settled back in his seat and waited for her to continue. He wanted to ease her concern, but perhaps after the way he had been avoiding her lately, he would have to earn back her trust.

"I didn't want to say anything until I was certain, and after that you seemed to need some time to yourself…"

He tensed but said nothing as he waited. He

wouldn't cut her off just yet, but heaven help him if she wanted to discuss Vaughan.

"I am with child. There is no question… the child is yours."

Mixed emotions battled within him. Sarah, the woman he cared for beyond anything or anyone else, was pregnant with his child. Elation rose within him like a swift tide. But that elation was inextricably mixed with more than a hint of dread. After all, she'd been up front in telling him that she would make sure he had his heir first before looking elsewhere for companionship.

"Say something," she said.

He realized that he must have been quiet for some time. Sarah was twisting her hands together in her lap, wrinkling the fabric of her dress.

He spoke carefully, not wanting to give voice to his doubts. "I'm pleased."

"You don't look happy. I thought you'd be overjoyed."

He remained silent, not wanting to ruin this moment with an argument. Sarah, however, had no qualms about continuing.

"I make you a solemn promise, James, that I won't be seeking the company of anyone else. I know you've come to expect the worst from me, but you should know that Robert's actions were entirely his own. He made overtures to me, but I no longer reciprocate his feelings."

His eyes met hers, words jamming in his throat.

When he didn't reply, she continued. "I intend to be faithful to my wedding vows. To you."

Relief, pure and blessed, poured through him. He didn't believe that his wife would lie just to ease his mind, not when she'd been so forthright with him before now. He wasn't sure what had caused her to change her mind but could no longer hold back his hope that Sarah was coming to care for him.

No longer content to wait, he moved to sit next to her. He didn't exactly pounce on her, but it was a near thing.

He dragged her onto his lap, his blood heating when she wrapped her arms around his neck and pressed her body against his. He took her mouth with his, and as always, she responded eagerly.

They spent the rest of the carriage ride home making up for having spent the previous two weeks apart. And, finally, Sarah fell asleep in his arms.

For the first time since he'd been forced to accept that his new bride loved someone else and hadn't wanted to marry him, James had hope for the future.

CHAPTER 14

SARAH COULDN'T SAY if she was happy exactly, but she was certainly content with the new state of her marriage. A week had passed since their return to Hathaway Park, and she and James had settled into a new peace.

She hadn't told him that she loved him, but assuring him that she intended to remain faithful seemed to be all he required from her. There were even times when she could almost convince herself that James cared for her.

Yes, she was content with her marriage.

Her maid was hovering over her, having just stripped her down to her chemise, when Sarah froze. Turning away from the other woman, she lifted the fabric and gazed at her thighs in horror.

"Is something the matter, my lady?" Alice asked as she came around to face her. Her gaze followed Sarah's and she gasped. "I thought you were with child?"

"I am," Sarah said, releasing her chemise to hide the sight of the blood. "Call for Dr. Reynolds, quickly!"

She watched Alice flee the room, standing in place a full minute. She tried to calm her racing heart as she moved to the bed, tossing the dress she'd worn onto its surface so she wouldn't stain the bedclothes. She frowned down at it, remembering how much James seemed to like that dress.

James found her several minutes later, rummaging through drawers, trying to remember where Alice kept the towels.

"Your maid told me that you needed the doctor."

She threw her hands up in the air then, losing the battle to keep her tears at bay. "I'm bleeding," she said, hating the tremor in her voice. "And I can't find a towel to place on the bed so I don't ruin the sheets…"

James swore, ignoring his wife's gasp as he lifted her off her feet and carried her to the bed.

"I'll buy you a whole new bed if need be, but you are not going to move from that spot until the doctor arrives."

His gaze moved down her form and she saw the color drain from his face. She didn't have the courage to look down again, afraid of what she'd see.

"I'm so sorry," she said before breaking down into sobs, barely able to catch her breath as she wondered if she was being punished in some way. It had taken her months to conceive, and now… Her mind shied away from finishing that thought.

James said nothing. What was there to say, after all?

But he lowered himself onto the side of the bed and pulled her against him, cradling her as she worked to control her fear.

She didn't know how long they stayed that way, but her tears had stopped when they finally heard a soft knock at the door.

James left her then and went to answer the door. She couldn't make out the muffled voices before James returned to her side.

"I'll be right outside while the doctor examines you," he said, leaning down to place a soft kiss on her forehead.

She knew he meant the words to be comforting, but she could see the concern in his eyes when he straightened to leave and couldn't help but feel that she had failed him.

JAMES HADN'T BEEN WAITING LONG, but each minute that passed seemed like an hour as he paced outside Sarah's bedroom. Her sobs had torn his heart in two, and he'd never felt more powerless in his life.

Finally the doctor stepped into the hallway, closing the door softly behind him.

He lacked the voice to ask, but his heart lifted when he saw the smile on the older man's face.

"Your wife is well," he said.

"And the baby?"

"I won't lie to you," Dr. Reynolds said. "Your wife is

at a very delicate time in her pregnancy. Some women have next to no symptoms during this time and are able to continue their routine with very little modification. But your wife is not one of them. For now, I see nothing to indicate that the pregnancy is in immediate danger. Some women bleed during these early months and reach the end of their confinement with no difficulty. But since we have no way of knowing whether that will be the case for Lady Hathaway, it is important that she rest as much as possible."

James felt as though a huge weight has been lifted from his chest. That feeling was short-lived, however, when the doctor continued.

"Lady Hathaway informed me that the two of you have been sharing a bed. Given the extra care your wife will need to ensure she carries this baby to term, I will have to insist that you forgo visiting her until we know that the health of her and her baby are no longer in danger."

The concern James had felt for his wife and unborn child was nothing compared to the guilt that settled over him now. His own selfish needs had caused this. If he had stayed away from Sarah, neither she nor the baby would be in danger now.

James hesitated outside his wife's bedroom door after the doctor had left. He didn't know what he was going to say to Sarah, but he had just steeled himself to face her when the door opened and her maid exited the room.

"My lord," she said with a quick curtsy before turning away.

"Wait," he said, stopping her. "How is she?"

"She's very tired. A good night's rest will do her wonders."

"Maybe I should leave her then."

"Oh no," she said with a quick shake of her head. "My lady is anxious to speak to you."

He gave her a curt nod and stepped through the door. Sarah was sitting upright in bed, and his remorse increased when he saw how pale and fragile she looked. He'd done that to her.

He approached the bed and lowered himself onto the edge, taking hold of one of her hands. It was so very cold.

"The doctor is optimistic," she said. "The bleeding has stopped, and he assured me that it looked more shocking than it actually was. Apparently some women are prone to bleeding early in their pregnancy—"

He silenced her with a soft kiss on her lips. He hated that she seemed to be blaming herself.

"It was my fault. I shouldn't have been so demanding of your attention. I assure you that it won't happen again."

Her shoulders slumped at his words. "I'm sorry."

He wanted to take her into his arms and just hold her, but they didn't have that type of relationship.

"Rest." Unable to resist, he placed a final kiss on her forehead and left the room.

CHAPTER 15

October 1813

IVE MONTHS HAD PASSED since Sarah's one and only bleeding episode. Five months since her relationship with James had come to a screeching halt.

Dr. Reynolds conducted his examination that morning, peppering her with questions about her level of activity. By his side stood the local midwife, Mrs. Bryers, who had been visiting her often to check on her progress.

When the doctor was done, Mrs. Bryers helped her back into a seated position and draped a bedsheet over her. Together, they waited for the doctor's pronouncement.

"I've seen nothing in this, or in my previous examinations, that gives me cause for concern. In my opinion, you are the picture of health."

Sarah hadn't been aware she was holding her breath until that moment. Air rushed out of her lungs, and she gripped the midwife's hand. "You are quite certain there is no danger to the baby?"

"No more than any other pregnancy. There is always a risk when a woman is increasing, you understand, but whatever caused you to bleed that one time, it is clear the danger is now well past."

"It's as we've told you," Mrs. Bryers said. "Sometimes women bleed in the early months but go on to have healthy babies. I've seen it many times myself."

Dr. Reynolds nodded. "Just so."

Calm settled over her at their reassurances. Everything was going to be fine. After her initial panic, she'd been certain her baby would be born healthy—she still believed that—but she'd been trying to mentally prepare herself for the worst.

Her thoughts went immediately to James. The doctor had still advised caution during his previous examinations, but his concern seemed to have passed. "Can my husband and I...?" She was too embarrassed to say the words. And if truth be told, she felt almost greedy asking the question. Surely it was too much to hope that everything would now fall into place for her and James.

The doctor smiled benevolently at her. "Yes, you can resume marital relations. If you'd like to rest now, I'll see if I can find him to tell him the good news. He's been very concerned for your well-being."

"Thank you so much, Dr. Reynolds." The words seemed inadequate.

The doctor turned to leave, and she tried to be patient while Mrs. Bryers fussed over her for a bit.

When the midwife finally left, she made her way downstairs. Her skin tingled. She couldn't wait to find James. Surely their marriage would now go back to normal. She was larger, but she knew from their past lovemaking that there were ways for a man and woman to be together where her size wouldn't be a hindrance.

James wasn't in his study, and when she asked the butler about his whereabouts, she was dismayed to learn that he'd gone out. She returned to her room, wondering if the doctor had spoken to him.

NEEDING to distract herself as she waited for James to return, Sarah decided to visit the dower house. The doctor had lifted the physical restrictions under which he'd placed her, yet she made sure to keep a leisurely pace. The twenty-minute walk stretched to half an hour, and a footman followed in case she needed assistance. She arrived at the smaller house flushed from the unaccustomed exertion yet happy at her newfound freedom.

She did, however, ask for a carriage to fetch her at the end of her visit. She didn't want to risk overexerting herself on her first day away from home in months.

It was midafternoon when she arrived home, and she was excited to learn that James had also returned.

She thanked the butler and proceeded to her bedroom, wanting to refresh her appearance before seeing him.

Nerves assailed her as she made her way upstairs. Their time apart had been a constant ache. At first she'd missed the physical side of their relationship most, but it didn't take her long to discover that what she really missed was *him*. All of him. The way he looked at her, how he went out of his way to check in with her throughout the day.

When she'd first started experimenting with the oil paints he'd given her at Christmas, he'd checked on her progress daily. He'd been there for her first few abysmal attempts, and when she'd finally started developing a feel for the new medium, the wonder on his face lifted her heart. She could almost feel his pride at those first modest accomplishments.

James was supremely confident most of the time, but now and again she'd caught a brief glimpse of uncertainty on his face. She hated that she'd caused that disquiet. She'd vowed to keep him at a distance, and for so long she'd succeeded. She wished now that she'd taken the advice of James's aunt and told him about her feelings. Because of her need to protect herself from being hurt, he'd withdrawn from her completely once they could no longer be intimate.

His absence had left a void in her heart. The only time she saw him now was over dinner, and more often than not his mother and sister were also present. He'd excuse himself once the meal was over, and she wouldn't see him again until the following evening.

She knew he wasn't sleeping in his bedroom, though she had heard him moving around during the day on occasion. It hadn't taken her long to start wondering if he was fulfilling his needs with another woman. Sharing the pleasures he used to share with her. He was, after all, a very physical man.

From there her thoughts had wandered into darker territory, imagining what would happen if another woman willingly shared more of herself than Sarah had been willing to give. It terrified her that he might come to love someone else.

Would James even want her now, given how large she'd become?

That thought had her hesitating outside her bedroom door, but only for a moment. Miranda Hathaway—no, she was Miranda Sanderson now—had been correct. She should have told James how she felt all those months ago. Now it might be too late.

Taking control of her wayward thoughts, Sarah straightened her shoulders and entered her bedroom. She would freshen up and then go in search of her husband.

She was reaching for the bellpull to summon her maid when the door to the dressing room that separated her bedroom from James's opened. Sarah spun around, her heart in her throat, expecting to see James. Instead, her maid rushed into the room. Startled, it took Sarah a few seconds to realize the importance of what she was seeing.

Alice was normally impeccable in her appearance, but

at that moment she could only be described as disheveled. She was trying to straighten her loosened hair as she took a few steps into the room but froze when she spotted Sarah. Her cheeks were flushed, her uniform wrinkled.

Sarah's heart stuttered. She turned away quickly. Her vision swimming with unshed tears, she reached for a bedpost to steady herself.

Alice rushed to her side and grasped her around the waist. "My lady, are you unwell? Should I call for the doctor?"

A bubble of hysterical laughter threatened to erupt at the question. The doctor had just told her that everything was perfect with her, only it wasn't. Her life was as far from perfect as possible.

"I turned too quickly," she said, unable to keep the slight tremor from her voice. "I am feeling a little lightheaded. Could you bring me something to eat?"

"Of course, my lady. What would you like?"

Sarah didn't think she'd be able to keep anything down just then, but she needed to get Alice out of the room. "Anything will do."

"I'll fetch something right away."

With a curtsy, her maid hurried from the room and Sarah let out a shaky breath. She tried to tell herself that she was jumping to conclusions and that Alice wouldn't betray her in that way. She knew her husband's sexual appetite was large, and it had been months since they'd last made love, but surely he wouldn't conduct an affair with her maid right under their roof.

She could try to find out.

Her gaze moved to the dressing room door, but she hesitated as she considered her next course of action. She could remain where she was, wait for Alice to return with something Sarah knew she wouldn't be able to eat. She could approach James another time, after her nerves had settled.

Or she could go through the dressing room to his bedroom and confront him.

Her head told her to take the first course of action, but her heart prevailed. She couldn't live with the uncertainty.

Her hands settled on her belly, and she took several deep breaths. Finally, her breathing somewhat steady, she dropped her hands, straightened her shoulders, and entered the dressing room.

It was empty, of course. Pressing forward lest she lose her nerve, she opened the second door and stepped into her husband's bedroom.

She'd been hoping to find it empty as well. Instead, her husband faced away from her while his valet stood behind him, a freshly starched cravat in his hands. On the bed lay a crumpled shirt and waistcoat.

He turned to face her, his freshly laundered shirt gaping open at the neck.

Her stomach dropped and her legs threatened to give way. Why would he be changing so early? Given the state her maid had been in when she'd exited the dressing room, Sarah could only think of one reason.

Words fled and she could only stare at him in silence, her heart aching.

James frowned. He motioned for his valet to continue, and the other man draped the fabric he was holding around James's neck and proceeded to tie the simple knot she knew her husband preferred.

"Did you wish to say something or just gawk at me?"

She flinched at the harshness of his tone. "I need to speak to you in private."

He said nothing and she waited. Dread was now a living, breathing thing inside her, and she had to wrestle with the almost overwhelming urge to turn and flee.

Fenton finished tying the knot and James dismissed him. When they were alone, he turned to face her. The expression on his face could only be described as forbidding.

Sarah hesitated as she considered what to say. How did one go about discussing the subject of resuming marital relations with one's husband? Despite what she now suspected to be true, she wanted... No, she needed to find a way back into her husband's affections. She told herself that Alice was merely a convenient diversion. If James was able to turn to his wife to satisfy his needs, he would have no use for the other woman.

She licked her lips, and he flinched before his scowl deepened. That small telltale sign that he wasn't immune to her gave her the courage to continue.

"The doctor was here this morning."

"I know."

"Did he... did he speak to you before he left?"

James hesitated, and for a moment she wasn't sure he was going to reply. Then he said simply, "Yes."

His admission surprised her. She'd assumed that the doctor hadn't had the opportunity to speak to him.

"So you know?"

He said nothing.

"You know that there is nothing to stop us from enjoying the relationship we had before he placed me on bed rest?"

"Yes, there is. Bedding you might hold only a small risk to our child's health, but it is a risk I am unwilling to take."

"But the doctor said there was no risk at all. I have been completely healthy since then. It's been months, and Dr. Reynolds said that if the baby was at risk, I would have continued to bleed."

He turned away from her, that small motion telling her more than words that he would not bend. And why should he? When faced with bedding his wife, who was as large as one of his horses, or his current mistress, what man wouldn't choose the latter?

Somehow she kept her voice from trembling when she continued. "I'm sorry to have disturbed you."

She managed to hold on to the shreds of her dignity as she exited the room through their shared dressing room. When her maid returned with something for her to eat, she feigned that she was asleep. She listened while the young woman placed the tray on her dressing table before quietly exiting the room. Only then did she allow her tears to fall.

HE'D MADE a horrible hash of things with Sarah, but James forced himself not to follow when she walked away from him. The only thing stopping him from plowing his hand into the wall was the knowledge that Sarah would hear it, and the last thing he wanted to do was to upset her even more than he'd already done.

Anger, directed mainly at himself, and frustration were his ever-present companions and he struggled daily to stay away from his wife. When he'd seen her standing in the dressing room doorway, he'd thought for a moment that he was dreaming.

It had taken every ounce of strength he possessed not to pull her into his arms and clutch her like a drowning man. Surely this was what it felt like to go insane. His nerves were frayed and his very skin felt too tight.

When she'd told him that she wanted to resume their lovemaking... He closed his eyes, feeling again the surge of lust that had risen within him. He'd been intentionally cold to her and hated himself for the hurt he'd seen in her eyes. But he'd needed to ensure she left before he caved and gave in to his baser urges. He vowed to make it up to her after their child was born. He only prayed it wouldn't be too late and that her feelings hadn't turned to hate before then.

CHAPTER 16

SARAH COULD BARELY stand to look at Alice, but she didn't confront the woman. What would she say? "By the way, are you sharing my husband's bed?" Nothing would be gained. After all, her husband wouldn't allow her to dismiss the woman who now warmed his bed.

It had been a week since she'd approached James, hoping to put an end to their estrangement. While it hardly seemed possible, she saw even less of him than before. She'd taken to having dinner in her room the past few days, unable to hide her low spirits from James's mother and sister while he remained absent.

A soft knock at the door signaled that her maid wished to collect her dinner tray. Sarah rose and steeled herself to betray none of her hurt.

Alice entered and dipped a brief curtsy before turning to remove the tray. She was so pretty it almost hurt Sarah to look at her. Tears began to sting her eyes, and she had to turn away. Instead of leaving with the tray, she heard Alice move behind her.

"My lady?"

Sarah took a couple of deep breaths and turned to face her maid.

"I need to tell you something, and I'm afraid you'll be unhappy."

A kick to her stomach would have hurt less than those words. "Perhaps we can just continue as we have been." They were the words of a coward, but Sarah wasn't sure she possessed the strength to have this conversation.

Alice frowned. "His Lordship said you would understand."

Sarah's legs threatened to give way, and she sat heavily on the edge of the bed. "This concerns my husband?"

Alice shook her head. "Not directly, no, but he does know about it."

A tiny spark of hope flickered to life within her. "So what you wish to discuss… it isn't about James?"

There was no mistaking the confusion on Alice's face. "No, my lady. I know I should have told you that day you saw me leaving the dressing room, but I was in such a state, and I couldn't be sure how you would react."

Sarah looked down into her lap where her hands were resting and noticed that they were shaking. She clutched them together to stop the trembling and looked back at her maid. "What did you wish to discuss?"

Alice swallowed heavily before replying. "My relationship with Fenton."

Sarah had to remind herself to breathe. "My husband's valet?"

Alice nodded. "We've..." She hesitated, and Sarah wanted to shake the words from her. But she waited while her maid visibly gathered her courage. "He's asked me to marry him."

Her words came out in a rush, and for a moment, Sarah thought she'd misunderstood her.

"So last week when you rushed into the room from the dressing room..."

Alice clenched her hands before replying. "We were having a romantic moment. But it wasn't something we'd planned. We've been very careful to make sure our relationship doesn't affect our work. I was putting away the new dresses that had arrived for you, and I think he was arranging His Lordship's cravats..."

Sarah could picture the scene. "And my husband entered his room then."

Alice nodded, clearly embarrassed. "I rushed in here, which you saw, and Fenton went out to attend to Lord Hathaway."

Relief swept over her, so intense that for a moment she found it difficult to breathe.

"I was afraid we'd both be dismissed from our positions, but Fenton spoke to His Lordship recently and he gave us his blessing. But you've been so out of sorts lately. I was afraid you'd learned of our relationship and disapproved."

This time it was Sarah's turn to be embarrassed. She should have known that James wouldn't betray her with her maid.

"When you rushed out of the dressing room, disheveled, and I saw my husband was in his bedroom, I'm afraid I jumped to the wrong conclusion."

The look of horror on the young woman's face was almost comical. "Oh no, my lady. How could you think I would do something like that? I would never betray you in such a way."

It wasn't wise, but Sarah needed to speak to someone about her feelings even if that someone was her maid. No doubt the entire household staff already knew that she and her husband were estranged, so it wasn't as though she'd be revealing any secrets.

"My pregnancy has been hard on our marriage. We've had to be apart, and you know how men are. They will find their amusements elsewhere. I apologize for thinking the worst of you, but when you came out looking as you did…"

"His Lordship cares for you. He wouldn't betray you."

Sarah glanced away and took a deep breath before replying. "I wish I could believe you, but his absences every night lead me to think otherwise."

Alice shook her head, her expression earnest. "No, my lady. It doesn't mean what you think. I didn't say anything earlier because it wasn't my place to intrude, but I believe you need to know the truth. His Lordship has spent every evening at home. He stays up late in his study and then retires to a bedroom in the guest wing. Fenton told me that your husband is concerned only about your health and has decided it is best if he stays away while you are increasing."

So many conflicting emotions rioted within her, she had to close her eyes for a moment. "No," she breathed.

Alice nodded. "It is true. The entire staff knows that His Lordship is devoted to you."

Sarah resisted the urge to laugh, knowing the sound would only come out tinged with bitterness. It appeared that the fates had played a cruel joke on her. How could the entire staff know her husband better than she did?

"There is one more thing," her maid said.

"And what is that?" Sarah prompted when Alice hesitated.

"Fenton told me this in confidence. He must never learn that I told you, but I feel it is vital you know."

Sarah managed to breathe evenly. "I promise no one will know."

Alice nodded. "His Lordship doesn't believe he is worthy of you. He thinks you are too good for him and that he did you a disservice in convincing your parents to allow him to marry you."

Sarah had never hated herself more than she did in that moment. She had done that to him. James was everything a woman could ever want in a husband. Certainly he was more a man than Robert had ever been. Yet, to protect herself from being hurt, she'd hidden the fact that she'd loved him almost from the beginning of their marriage.

She stood and squared her shoulders, prepared to do battle with her stubborn, too-good-to-be-believed husband. "Where is Lord Hathaway right now?"

CHAPTER 17

HER CONVERSATION WITH ALICE played over and over in her mind. She still couldn't believe she'd thought he was spending his nights with her maid when, in fact, he'd been hiding from her in a different part of the house. All because he cared for her and wanted to ensure her safety.

With the clarity of hindsight and with a light shone on all the dark, suspicious places in her mind, it all made sense to her now. She remembered just how stricken he'd been when she bled early in her pregnancy. Since that day, she'd convinced herself that he'd cared only about keeping his potential heir safe and that he'd decided to relieve his very healthy sexual appetite elsewhere. But she'd misjudged him in every way possible.

The fact that he believed himself unworthy of her was so far from the truth it almost hurt to contemplate. Her heart clenched as she acknowledged that she had been the cause of that. She'd convinced herself that all men were like her father and like Robert—selfish and only concerned about themselves. And in her zealous desire to protect herself from being hurt, she'd in turn hurt a man who had done nothing to deserve such treatment. In the end, she'd only succeeded in making both herself and her husband unhappy.

James... the man she loved.

She had to go to him, to tell him—and to show him—that she cared for and desired him above all other men. And God help her, she'd even bare her own heart and confess her love. It was more than she deserved that he'd love her, but she would learn to be content to have their relationship return to how it had been before everything had fallen apart.

She wrapped herself in her dressing gown and made her way down the dark hallways to his study. At six months of pregnancy, she feared she was beginning to waddle. But she'd occasionally caught the heated glances he cast her way when he hadn't started to avoid her completely, giving her hope that he still found her desirable. Her greatest problem, however, would be overcoming his reluctance to act on that desire.

Feeling more certain about her course of action than she'd ever been in her life, she knocked on his study door and waited for his permission to enter. When it came, she gathered her resolve about her like a cloak—knowing that her husband would do everything in his power to send her away—and entered the room.

James was sitting at his desk, his elbows on the

surface and his head cradled in his hands. He looked the picture of defeat, and words failed her.

When she didn't speak, he looked up. His eyes widened in surprise when he saw her. He rose swiftly, his eyes darting to her belly. "Is something amiss with the baby?"

"No, everything is fine," she said, rushing to reassure him. His shoulders sagged with relief and she took a moment to close the door behind her. "In fact, that is exactly what I wished to discuss with you."

His brows drew together. "I don't understand."

She crossed to his desk and skirted around it until she was standing next to him. She didn't miss the fact that his hands were clenched at his sides. Before that evening, she would have assumed he was annoyed with her, but given Alice's revelations, she now believed he was trying to keep himself in check. To keep from reaching out for her. That small proof of his emotions caused hope to surge within her.

"I haven't had a bleeding episode in months, and the doctor believes the danger to my pregnancy has passed."

He looked away from her and raised a hand to massage one temple. "We've already had this discussion. There is nothing more to be said."

She had to take a deep breath and gather her courage before she could continue. "I need to know why you haven't returned to my bed."

He dropped his hand and turned away from her.

"James?"

He shook his head. "I cannot discuss this with you."

169

"Cannot? Or will not?"

"Both."

She moved closer and reached for his hand. Placing it on her rounded belly, she watched as his expression softened. His hand curled over her middle, the warmth of his touch seeping through her nightdress and dressing gown.

"And what if I don't accept that?"

He lifted his face to gaze into her eyes and she saw, reflected in their depths, the pain he was suffering.

"I was selfish before and put our child's life at risk. Put *your* life at risk. I won't do that again."

She could tell by the tightness of his jaw and the determined glint in his eye that he wouldn't be swayed from his decision. But if James had taught her anything, it was that there were ways for a man and woman to be together that would pose no risk to her or to their baby.

"I miss you," she said.

He held her gaze, his eyes seeming to burrow straight through her, but he didn't reply. She would have to press the matter, and she knew just how to do it. She'd offer him the one thing she knew he'd wanted to experience with her but that she had always been too shy to even contemplate. Remembering again how selfless he had been on the first night of their marriage, she vowed to do the same for him now. She would show her husband that she placed his pleasure above her own.

But first she had to make sure he wouldn't pull away.

She feigned a swoon and he caught her upper arms, holding her steady. Sarah leaned into him, making sure to press her breasts against his chest. His sharp intake of breath gave her all the additional strength she needed to continue.

"I think I need to sit down." She didn't have to feign the breathlessness in her voice.

He led her the few steps to his study chair, released her, and frowned down at her. "Have you eaten? Should I ring for your maid?"

Before he could escape, she reached for his hand and tugged him closer. He came, stopping when his legs brushed against hers, but didn't hide his reluctance. Somehow she managed to suppress the smile of satisfaction that threatened to undermine her plan.

"I know you feel strongly about this, so I won't try to change your mind."

He visibly relaxed, but she could tell he would like nothing better than for her to leave. He'd been avoiding her for months, but that was going to end tonight.

"I'll see you to your bed," he said. When she raised a brow, he squeezed his eyes shut and blew out a breath. "Not like that."

"I know, James. You are far too noble."

He released a snort of derision. She hated that he doubted his own worth.

"I want to give you pleasure like you did for me on the first night of our marriage and on so many other nights since then."

He couldn't hide the effect her words had on him as a shudder went through him. "You needn't make the sacrifice—"

She could see that he was already hard with desire. He was trying to act the gentleman, but his body betrayed him. She placed her hand over the solid length of his arousal and was gratified when she felt him twitch at her boldness.

He shook his head, but when she started to undo the buttons, he didn't stop her.

"I want to do this. I *need* to do this."

She pulled down the placket covering the front of his trousers and drew out his hard length. She'd missed this more than she'd thought possible. Missed being uninhibited with her husband, being able to touch him anywhere she wanted. And the way he looked down at her—a combination of disbelief and awe on his face—told her he felt the same way.

She stroked up and down his hard length just the way she knew he liked. Although he had proposed it on more than one occasion, she'd never taken him into her mouth, so he wouldn't expect her to do so now. And given their current estrangement, she knew he wouldn't suggest it.

He was standing before her while she remained seated, and she only had to shift forward a little to bring her mouth against him.

"Sarah." Her name was a ragged whisper, an unspoken plea that urged her to continue.

She wasn't sure if she was doing it correctly, but she knew how he liked her to run her hands up and down his hardness. She imagined that she needed to mirror that motion with her mouth.

His fingers threaded through her hair, his hands tightening against her head, but he allowed her to remain in control as she moved up and down his length. He was too big to fit all the way into her mouth, so she grasped the base of his hardness with one hand, stroking him with both her hand and her mouth while she used her other hand to fondle him below. When he groaned, excitement shot through her own body. Why had she been so reluctant to do this for him before today?

"Sarah, I can't… I'm going to finish."

He tried to move her head away from him, but she resisted. She wanted this, both for herself and for him. To show James that she accepted him.

He spent himself into her mouth with a guttural sound, and she swallowed all of it. She allowed him to pull her away from him then, watching in silence as he covered himself and buttoned the fall of his trousers. Then she stood to face him.

His eyes searched hers for several seconds. "Why?" he finally asked.

"Because I hate this distance between us, and…"

"And?" he prompted when she hesitated.

She'd come this far and she wouldn't allow fear to continue to silence her. She lifted a hand to caress his cheek. "I love you and I cannot continue to live separate from you. And since I'm being completely honest—perhaps for the first time since our marriage began—I'm afraid you'll find someone else to take my place."

He shook his head in disbelief. "I must have fallen asleep. Surely this is a dream."

He spread his arms and she moved into his welcoming embrace.

"You're not dreaming."

"In the face of your honesty, you should know that I'd wait forever for you. I love you, Sarah Hathaway, and no one else could ever take your place."

She would have wept with joy if her husband hadn't chosen to distract her then in another, more delicious manner.

EPILOGUE

January 1814

$\mathcal{A}$LL TOO SOON, James found himself pacing outside Sarah's bedroom again. Only this time, instead of worrying that she might be miscarrying, his wife was giving birth to their first child.

His mother had tried to drag him away, advising him that Sarah might be some time yet. James knew he wouldn't be able to stop obsessing over how Sarah and their child were doing. And so he planted himself outside her door and refused to allow anyone to draw him away. If he'd been allowed, he would have been in the room with her.

Her screams had him itching for a bottle of brandy, but he wouldn't dishonor her in that way. Sarah was going through the pain of childbirth... his part, by comparison, was easy. Still, he hated that he could only stand helplessly by and wait.

The door opened a crack and Lady Mapleton poked her head out, giving him a strained smile that didn't quite reach her eyes.

"The baby is almost here," she said before closing the door again and disappearing.

He knew that Sarah's mother was only trying to be helpful, but her words did little to put him at ease. He'd been present for the birth of many foals, and he knew that the danger to the mother didn't always ease after the baby was born. Complications did arise. He personally knew two men whose wives had given birth to healthy children only to then succumb to death when they continued to bleed.

The sound of a baby's cry pierced the air, and James collapsed against the wall. He closed his eyes and prayed that Sarah would also be well.

A touch on his arm had him opening his eyes to find Emily and his mother standing before him. The expression on his mother's face told him that despite her attempts to calm his nerves, she'd also been concerned.

"It will be over soon," his mother said.

Emily's face was pale, and for once, she wasn't her normal jubilant self.

"I had no idea childbirth could go on for so long or that it was so painful. I'm glad now that I wasn't allowed inside the room with Sarah. As it is, I don't think I'll want to have children… not if the screaming is any indication of the pain I'll have to suffer."

Emily shuddered and his mother laughed. "You'll

forget all about Sarah's screams after you've held the baby."

Emily looked doubtful, but the bedroom door opening prevented her from replying.

Mrs. Bryers beamed at him. "You have a healthy son."

"Sarah?" he asked, holding his breath.

"Her Ladyship is tired, but she, too, is well. She wants to see you now."

James needed no further prodding, brushing past the midwife and making his way to Sarah's side. His wife was gazing down at the baby in her arms, an expression of wonder on her face. After tearing his gaze from her face, he realized she was feeding the baby at her breast.

He lowered himself onto the bed beside her, ignoring the bustle of movement around him. "You look beautiful," he said, cupping her cheek.

Her laugh warmed his heart. "You are decidedly prejudiced. I'm sure I look a fright."

She looked down at their son and he followed suit. He couldn't resist moving his hand to cradle the baby's head, marveling at his warmth. His son continued suckling, ignoring his touch.

He had no words in that moment. He wanted to tell Sarah what she meant to him, but the words lodged in his throat—that he would never again doubt her or their life together. That he would do everything in his power to make her happy.

Fortunately, his wife knew him well enough that no words were necessary.

"I know," she said, leaning forward to brush a kiss against his lips.

The squawk of protest from their son had her leaning back, frantically trying to reattach him to her breast. James's heart swelled.

There, in front of him, was everything he'd ever need.

Thank you for reading *Lord Hathaway's New Bride*. If you enjoyed this book, you can share that enjoyment by recommending it to others and leaving a review.

To learn when Suzanna has a new release, you can sign up to receive an email alert at http://www.suzannamedeiros.com/newsletter/.

To read more about the author's books and learn where you can buy copies, you can visit the "Books" page on the author's website: http://www.suzannamedeiros.com/books/

Book 3 in the *Hathaway Heirs* series, *The Captain's Heart*, is available now. For a sneak peek, turn the page...

EXCERPT—THE CAPTAIN'S HEART

When the man who saves his life during the Battle of Waterloo dies from wounds that were meant for him, Captain Edward Hathaway must live with the guilt of having survived and is determined to fulfill that man's dying wish.

Grace Kent only accepted her childhood friend's proposal of marriage so he wouldn't go off to war with a broken heart. But while she still grieves for her friend after learning of his death, she cannot resist her attraction to the handsome Captain Hathaway.

He is determined to discharge his duty at the expense of his own happiness. She wants only one taste of true passion. Together, can they overcome the guilt that continues to haunt them both?

The Captain's Heart is a *Hathaway Heirs* novella and was formerly available in *The Incomparables* box set.

GRACE MOVED SILENTLY through the house and exited by means of a window in her father's study. Helen had already gone to bed, exhausted from having risen early that morning and spending hours in a carriage. That left Grace free to slip out of the house shortly after the sun went down. She couldn't risk trying to saddle a horse herself and being caught, so she set out on foot in the direction of the village.

It took her three quarters of an hour to reach the cottage the captain had mentioned he'd be renting for the remainder of his stay in Somerset. When she finally arrived, her stomach was in knots. She could very well imagine what Hathaway's servant—surely he'd have at least one with him—would think when he found an unescorted woman paying a call after dark.

She almost sagged with relief when the door was opened by Hathaway himself. Surprise, then delight, lit his face when he saw her. He glanced over her shoulder and his smile turned into a frown.

"Please tell me you didn't arrive on foot?"

She couldn't resist the urge to dip into a deep curtsy, saying, "It is very nice to see you too, Captain."

For a moment she thought he was going to lecture her about safety, but in the end, his good humor won out. He opened the door even wider, and she stepped into the hallway.

"I'd offer you refreshments, but…" He gave a small shrug. "I only have my valet with me and he has gone out."

Hathaway's words set one small part of her mind at ease. At least he didn't have scores of servants who would immediately brand her a trollop.

They were alone in the house, and her pretense was now at an end. Grace took a deep breath to steady her nerves and met his gaze. There was no point moving to the small sitting room she spied on the right. Once he learned the truth, the captain would give her Freddie's letter, and she would be on her way again.

"I am here to let you know my sister arrived this afternoon." She hesitated, dreading what she must confess now.

Hathaway nodded. "I'll call tomorrow then."

Somehow she had to tell him the truth. "About that, there is something I must tell you. I—" She froze when Hathaway placed a finger over her lips.

"Let me speak first."

The way he was looking at her, the fact that his hand had moved and now he was cupping her face, rubbing his thumb over her lower lip, left her bereft of speech. She could only nod.

"Once my duty here is discharged, I will be leaving."

She waited, knowing he wanted to say more.

"I don't want to waste what little time we have together talking about your sister. I would much rather talk about you and me."

He stepped closer so their bodies were almost touching and she found it difficult to breathe. She could see the heat in his eyes as he gazed down at her, trying to tell her without words just what he wanted from her.

She wanted the same thing.

ABOUT THE AUTHOR

Suzanna Medeiros was born and raised in Toronto, Canada. Her love for the written word led her to pursue a degree in English Literature from the University of Toronto. She went on to earn a Bachelor of Education degree, but graduated at a time when no teaching jobs were available. After working at a number of interesting places, including a federal inquiry, a youth probation office, and the Office of the Fire Marshal of Ontario, she decided to pursue her first love—writing.

Suzanna is married to her own hero and is the proud mother of twin daughters. She is an avowed romantic who enjoys spending her days writing love stories.

She would like to thank her parents for showing her that love at first sight and happily ever after really do exist.

To learn more about Suzanna's books, you can visit her website at
http://www.suzannamedeiros.com
or visit her on Facebook at

http://www.facebook.com/AuthorSuzannaMedeiros.

To learn when she has a new release available, you can sign up for her new release mailing list at http://www.suzannamedeiros.com/newsletter.

BOOKS BY SUZANNA MEDEIROS

Dear Stranger

Forbidden in February (A Year Without a Duke)

The Novellas: A Collection

Landing a Lord series

Dancing with the Duke

Loving the Marquess

Beguiling the Earl

The Unaffected Earl — Coming Soon

The Unsuitable Duke — Coming Soon

Hathaway Heirs series

Lady Hathaway's Indecent Proposal

Lord Hathaway's New Bride

The Captain's Heart

For more information, please visit the "Books" page on the author's website:

http://www.suzannamedeiros.com/books/

Made in the USA
Las Vegas, NV
20 September 2021